POPPY HIVES

a novel

Chris Blaine

ISBN: 978-1-959563-36-5

Maudlin Pond Press
P.O. Box 53
Tybee Island, GA 31328
www.maudlinpond.com

Printed in the United States of America

For Sally

CHAPTER ONE

There were never any days during which Bartholomew Rombert had to pass the time away in solitude. He had a full complement of farm animals which keep him busy. Each had a name and a personality. They required feeding, pasturing, monitoring of the birthing process, and protection from the elements and predators. Occasionally, one would require his nursing if it became injured or sick. He tended a garden of vegetables and a small orchard of fruit. He planted and tended the feed for his stock. He never lacked for companionship or a need to rise early and work all day.

There were occasional dogs, lost in the meandering scent trails, which approached and familiarized themselves with a sniff at his cuffed coveralls or barked insecurely from a distance. There had been all types of dogs - mostly beagles and hounds - which punctuated the weeks as they came and went on their solitary journeys. Some he fed; some he didn't. If they had a friendly face, perhaps a collar and weren't too large, he would give them a meal of grits mixed with bacon drippings. Some would eagerly lap it up; others would pace around the white porcelain dish curiously wondering if the strange concoction was familiar and edible. Inevitably, they would look up at him with eyes begging for his approval as though waiting for a blessing. He would speak a kind word to relax their perked ears and assuage their fears.

Before becoming acclimated to their new environment, they might cower under the cabin in the cool darkness, listening to the footsteps and strange sounds above. Mostly they slept, rested, and healed wounds for several days. He didn't bother them because they weren't bothering him. They would venture into the daylight when he left the cabin and would slake their thirst at the stream, stopping only to spray a tree or fencepost along the way. At night when the curious human sounds were quieted, they would ease from their security and move about in search of more food from the cracked porcelain dish and elsewhere on the grounds.

The more domesticated would recline at the porch door where the aroma of food was most prevalent. He would not feed them because they got in his way. They had become excessively dependent upon their master and had no semblance of independent dispositions. They were too familiar and begged. He believed in the survival of the fittest. He had never begged for his survival, so must they.

At other times, Bartholomew's companion was his shadow. The constant presence was his only reminder that he was alive. On overcast days, even this faithful tagalong would abandon him.

During the fall of the year he had to be on alert. Hunters wandered into his sanctuary on foot hoping to catch a deer in an idle graze. He would run in the direction of their shots. Sometimes he would cross paths with a frightened deer or feral hog. He would tell the hunter he was trespassing on his property without his permission. He never armed himself. At times he would be shot at by the hunter as he moved through the underbrush. When he confronted the hunter, he would confiscate any animals poached and demand that the hunter immediately leave. Permission was never granted to hunt his property.

To him, hunters were thieves. They could not afford the price of land, so they usurped the privilege of others. To him, poaching was the sin of coveting. He vigorously defended his ownership rights. They had no cause to invade his privacy other than to needlessly kill defenseless animals.

The wildlife was accustomed to Bartholomew's coming and going. They paid each other little attention. Neither ran nor flew for cover in fear of the other. That is what made them such easy game for the poachers. Regularly in the early morning hours, the deer would wander onto his yard grass and nibble at the fresh shoots. They were damn near pets and provided sporadic company when there were no dogs around to run them off. Besides, they were beautiful creatures. He would harvest them when he was in need of meat. That is why God had given them to him: to hold, protect, and, when the time came, use for his own sustenance. The wild animals were like a crop of corn in the field. He ate some, fed some to his stock, and took some to the grist mill for credits. There was a time for everything, and everything had its time, use and purpose in the cycle of life.

Although Bartholomew had an old Remington breach-loading rifle, a relic passed along from father to son after the Civil War, he preferred hunting with bow and arrow. There were several reasons. He could recycle the arrows; whereas cartridges, he couldn't. But most important, the arrow made no loud and sudden noise to frighten the animals. An arrow whizzing by could be the flight of a bird or a fallen tree bough. He could always reload and launch a second arrow. On the other hand, he really didn't trust the rifle; it was, as he put it, a machine with moving parts. It could misfire or not fire at all. The rifle could explode, as he had often been told in his youth, and do more harm to him than to the intended prey. He seldom took the Remington off the pegs above the door.

Once or twice a black bear would try to rob his beehive or attack the chicken coop. He would casually approach the animal and discharge a blast above its head. The bear would scamper back into the woods from which it came and seldom returned. Now and then, some stranger would come to the house. He didn't trust strangers. Twice a marauder attempted to rob Bartholomew, thinking he had a hoard of gold coins. They acted really friendly and told Bart what a nice place he had, but sooner or later they would get down to business and ask questions about money.

They would try to estimate his acreage in crops and ask what they would bring at market. They were taking the measure of him. Bartholomew would be evasive and say he only had enough to keep him and Daisy, his plow mule, going from year to year. Bart would say he bartered for what he needed, other than what he could raise on his own, so there was never any cash that traded hands. Bart kept one hand on the rifle. Usually, the unwanted visitor would pull a Bible from a pocket and begin to spout passages on one subject or another. One pulled a long blade knife instead of a Bible. Bart jabbed the man in the chest with the bore of the Remington so quickly the man was knocked onto his backside. Bart stood back at arm's length with the Remington pointed at the visitor's face. "Fella, you best be going now or you're gonna to be wearing a hole in your head where your face should be."

Bart hated the way people hid behind Bibles or in the phrase, "In the name of the Lord." He had some experience in church-going matters back when he was courting. Mostly, his experiences were because of his sparking with Eugenia on the grounds of the Solid Rock Primitive Baptist Church out on the Old Plank Road near Davisville over by Big Top Mountain.

Most womenfolk kept about the house, tending to their ritual of duties. But Eugenia was different; she was born into the milling business. She was an only child, the product of a difficult birth that left her mother weak and sickly-like. Back when she was a young 'un and when the corn or wheat needed grinding, her daddy needed her at the mill. She wore overalls like a man and dipped tobacco. Although she hadn't had much schooling, Eugenia could read and cipher numbers better than most of the farmers coming to mill their crops. Bart took a shine to her right off.

Bartholomew was timid and inexperienced in the wooing of the opposite sex. His tongue got tied in a knot and twisted like braided rope when he tried to say something nice. The more he tried to converse, the more his face reddened. He bathed and bought a new plaid shirt and overalls so she would think him to be successful. He felled trees, pulled stumps and planted more corn and winter wheat in the year following, darn near killing Daisy in the process. The animal was fit but wasn't accustomed to working the four extra nights a month when the moon was full and the skies were clear. He wanted to impress Eugenia with the bounty from his ardor.

"How many loads you bringin'?" she asked.

"I expect maybe twenty more."

"Lordy! How many acres you got planted?"

"I'd say better than fifty."

"You do all your own work?"

"Yeah. I could assist the neighbors, and then they'd come help me with the harvest, but I'd rather do it myself than have all those people about the place. Besides they'd expect to be fed and watered." Turning the conversation back to being a bachelor, "Without a wife, I couldn't return the favor in like."

"Where's all your womenfolk at?"

"Dead and gone. Been that a way. There's only me and my mule."

Bartholomew took credits instead of cash. There was a big recession in the country, and nobody had money to pass about in bill-paying. He didn't know who was president and didn't really care as long as the government and big city folk left him alone. His credits were good everywhere, even with Palmer at his dry goods store where he could trade for supplies. Bart would visit about every other month and hear the news of the nation. He never voted or cared anything about political parties and only understood half of what was told.

"You going to Big Sunday at Solid Rock?" Eugenia asked Bart.

"What day would that be?" he asked.

"Well, today's Tuesday. So, that would be in five days."

"What's it all about? Is it a revival or something?" he asked.

"No. We had that back in the first week of September. Big Sunday is when we pound the preacher," she answered.

"Never been to a poundin'. You best explain on the subject."

"Everybody brings a pound of something as a gift for the preacher. Mostly, we bring Mason jars of fruit or vegetables that will keep over winter. There will be all kinds of sweet cakes and pies, hams all dressed up, potatoes, yams, corn fixed every which way; you've never seen so much food except at a wedding. You eat like a hog till you gotta loosen your belt."

Bart thought about a hot apple pie with a cinnamon taste. His mouth began to moisten from the memory of one he had many years before. When Eugenia spoke the word wedding, the thought of marriage and intimacy blushed Bart's face.

"I'd sure like some apple pie or a cobbler," Bart remarked.

"All you got to do is show up for the preaching before the pounding."

"About when does it start?"

"Before high noon. This ain't no Easter sunrise affair. You got you a Bible? Iffen you don't, I got an extra 'un." Eugenia had no intention of being with a heathen soul. A man had to have religion, and that came from regular churchin'.

"I got my mother's."

"You ever read it?"she queried him.

"I don't do much at readin'. But I tried once to study the book." Bart looked about to see if anybody was listening to their conversation. He whispered, "There are so many words that I'm not sure of the meaning." Bart was being open and honest with Eugenia. She was askin', and he was a-tellin'. He would have avoided the subject if a man had asked. A man's personal is nobody's business but his own.

"You bring it along with you. When the preacher says, 'turn to Corinthians1: 13,' do you know what he means?"

Bartholomew looked down dejectedly at his worn shoes and pushed out his lower lip. "No."

Triumphantly, Eugenia said, "Don't worry, I can help you find the right page."

"Would you really?" Bartholomew knew that meant he could not only sit on the same pew, but would be standing next to Eugenia sharing a Bible. He had never been that social to a girl as far as he could recall. The thought of his body touching near her kept him awake all night and caused him countless flushes. Thoughts of Eugenia filled his mind for five days until he was about sick with nervousness.

Bart unstrapped Daisy from the wagon harness and tied her to a post rail near some fine buggy horses. Hay had been spread for feed. He saw how pitiful his swaybacked, floppy-eared mule looked in comparison to the well-bred stallions and mares. He became self-conscious with the thought of himself being a mule among refined and learned people such as the Palmers. His hopes and pride had been all but washed out when he heard a loud whistle from the church opening. There stood Eugenia in a dress waving an impatient hand for him to hurry up to her.

"Where you been all day?" she asked. "I've been here all morning waiting on you. Did you bring your Bible?"

"Oh, I left it in the wagon."

"Well, go fetch it. The preaching is about to commence. I've got a place saved for us up near the front."

Bart ran back to his buggy. "What 'bout the pound uh honey?" he yelled.

"Leave it be till after the preaching. Now come on."

When they walked into the church, the congregation was standing and singing the first stanza of "How Great Thou Art" accompanied by Ed Watson pushing and pulling on an accordion. The people seemed to sway with his movements. Thankfully, the accordion helped to drown the squeak in Bart's loose shoe sole. Bart was very conscious of his shoes and wished he had taken them off at the door. He tried to make his steps keep in time with the organ so that the squeak would be buried as a disharmonic note. Eugenia tugged at him and looked at his noisy shoe with an unapproving glare. He felt as conspicuous as a rooster crowing in a hen house.

Not only was there the unfamiliar sound of the accordion, there were also the strange scents of perfume, toilet water, and colognes that saturated the air. Bart took to a fit of sneezing during a prayer that drew everyone's attention. He had left his nose rag at the cabin and had to resort to wiping his face with his sleeve. Finally, Eugenia offered her handkerchief to stifle his sound. She was more of a lady than her guest was a gentleman. She almost felt as though she had a child with her on the pew bench rather than a near-grown man. She said "Amen" just a little louder than Bart thought she should have and followed with an elbow jabbed to his ribs.

During Reverend Allston Henslowe's preaching, Bart fired off a few more sneezes like gun shots. With each sneeze, an elderly lady seated in the pew before him would jump, then bring a hand to the back of her head and smooth her hair into place. She had bangle wrist bracelets that clattered. Later, when Henslowe's preaching was over, she gave him the most insolent look she could muster without fear of being damned for the sin of not loving a neighbor.

Eugenia's father, Cyrus Boyd, shared the pine pew and quietly sat to her right. Bart had the aisle seat and was able to stretch his feet between the pews. During the preaching, Cyrus' eyelids began to flicker. His head bobbed. He was on the brink of dozing off when Eugenia gave him an elbow jab. When he was thus abruptly startled, he let out a loud yelp to which nearly half the congregation joined in an echo of "Amens" and "Hallelujahs." The preacher was expounding on the miracle of Christ's feeding the multitude with a few fish and loaves of bread. Eugenia deduced he was anticipating the bounty of his own harvest following the morning worship.

Bartholomew shook the hands of the menfolk and bowed graciously to the ladies before filling his plate with a grand assortment of goodies. He was used to eating when he was hungry and not waiting for a long-winded preacher to bless every can, dish, plate, platter, and cup of green apple-cider punch. He ate from the desserts first, which, according to Eugenia's scolding, was the reverse of proper etiquette. He had consumed half an apple pie before she had made him aware of the social custom of certain foods being eaten before others.

"What difference does it make? It all ends up in the same place."

"Proper etiquette is to eat soup, salad, fish, meat, fruit, then sweets."

"Are you sure of that? It seems awfully strange. Are you making this up?"

"No. I'm not. Watch some of the others if you don't believe me. See if they eat the sweets before the meats. One before the other is poor for digestion," Eugenia advised.

"I can't see a whole lot from where I'm a perched. I'll walk about a bit on the way to the cider and observe as I go along."

"Wait. I'll go with you. Isn't there something you can do about that squeaky shoe?"

"I could pour some water in it. That would quiet it down a might bit."

"No. That's quite all right. I can live with the shoe the way it is rather than have you drip water with every step. Everybody will think you have a hole in your shoe."

"I don't neither."

"It was just a matter of… never you mind. Do you see everyone eating meat and vegetables?" Eugenia asked.

"Yeah. But I don't think they know what they're missing. The goodies might be all gone by the time they get to them."

Eugenia chided, "If you want to fit in, you do what others are doing, which, I might add, is not eating dessert first. Now, will you promise me you'll behave?"

"If you'n ashamed of me, maybe I oughta eat out back where nobody can see my manners or hear my shoe squeak?"

"Don't be absurd!"

"I'm being truthful. Did you see the look that woman gave me when the preaching ended?"

"No. I didn't."

"I could feel the darts coming out of her eyes striking me dead. I never saw a look like that mean before. Are all these people Christians, or are they just learning how?"

"Oh, it's time to pound the preacher. Quick! Run and

fetch your honey from the wagon."

When Bart returned with his honey and stood by Cyrus and Eugenia. Cyrus Boyd took his turn and stepped into the circle saying, "Ladies and gentlemen of Solid Rock Primitive Baptist Church, it is my esteemed pleasure to present to you Mister Bartholomew Rombert."

Eugenia whispered, "Place your honey on the table." Bart hesitated.

Everybody clapped except the old woman who was seated in a pew in front of Bart at the preaching. She was intolerably unforgiving of his trespassed sneezes and would not rain praise upon him.

Bart's face was crimson. He could feel it pulsate. Eugenia nudged him toward the table where the food was piled. Everybody clearly heard his shoe squeak. The children laughed and pointed at his foot. Bart wanted to crawl into the darkest corner under his cabin and hide like a stray dog. He stopped before the table and placed his jar of golden honey among the clusters of fruits and vegetables in similar jars. He paused, then turned. He had to walk ten feet back. He took a step. Squeak went his shoe. The kids were howling in laughter. Bart's head drooped; he thrust his hands in his side pockets. Eugenia stepped forward and took him by the arm and brought him back and continued out the door.

"I'm ready to go home now," he said. "They had their fun."

"And the apple pie. Was it as good as you remembered?"

Bart's face gradually lifted, and a smile matching Eugenia's spread across his face. "Yes, it certainly was."

"So, it was worth coming?" she asked.

"It was worth comin' even if there wasn't apple pie. Thank you for askin' me. You are a nice person, and I'll always think of you with kindness." He lifted his hand to his heart as though he were saluting the flag of the nation, then turned and left.

"Maybe, I'll see you at the mill?"

"Maybe."

CHAPTER TWO

The humiliation of Solid Rock Primitive Baptist Church burned at Bartholomew for several months. He dwelled on the thought of the congregation laughing at him. It was a stain that wouldn't wash out. He thought they had been cruel and hurtful, paying more attention to his shoes than to his heart and soul. "After all," he thought, "they hadn't given me the first chance. Not a one of them, exceptin' Eugenia, even tried to know the person in those squeaky shoes. They ought to be made to walk in my shoes for a day and see what it's like. Then they would stop their laughing."

Bart decided that he wouldn't give them a second chance. He traded some mill credits for a new pair of shoes and some men's handkerchiefs at Palmer's.

"I'm pleased you came to church for the pounding. It was an honor to have you visiting," Seth said earnestly. He had felt Bart's degradation of being poor and ill equipped. His kind words eased Bart's apprehension slightly. The shoes and handkerchief were left in the wrappings and placed under the bed as though they were Christmas presents waiting to be brought out on the biggest day of the year. They were precious gifts he was giving to himself.

Bartholomew cut, thrashed, dried, and bagged his winter wheat, as he had his corn, by himself. He had twice the crop of the previous year, requiring numerous wagon trips to the mill with Daisy. Eugenia was not at the mill on his first day's haul or on the second. He signed the papers for the amount Cyrus was willing to pay. Prices were still down because nobody had money except the federal government. They named their price, which made Bart's wage equivalent to twenty-five cents a day for his labor. There wasn't another mill within a day's ride. Daisy wasn't up to plowing and hauling. She needed her rest time.

Bart asked one of the hands about Eugenia and was told she was prostrate with the grippe. Cyrus told Bart he and Eugenia had enjoyed having him attend the Pounding Sunday, even though the preacher turned out to be a rascal.

Cyrus explained, "The morning after we pounded him, he took off with all the food, offerings, and the money for the building fund. He sold the food at Palmer's place for cash money and got better than twenty dollars, him being a preacher and all. Not even the horse and buggy belong to him. I just don't know what to say about these men of the cloth. You just can't trust them."

"Maybe, he was called into a mission by the Lord?"

"He had only one mission and it was himself. I just feel so terrible about all the people that put their trust in him. And him passing as a man of God. He violated them! If he ever shows his face around these parts again, a rope will be waiting for him." Cyrus was spitting mad as he spoke. The veins in his neck were swollen. "And them making fun of your shoes when they were praising the preacher with gifts. What makes them so holy?"

Wishing he had not visited the church, Bartholomew wanted the conversation to take a change in direction. "And how is the Miss Martha doing?"

"I'm afraid she might catch the grippe from Eugenia. Aunt Carlotta from over to Springford is taking care of them both. She's my wife's mother's sister. That's why we call her Aunt. She's like the nurse of the family. I sent for her day before yesterday. Her sisters Beulah, Eula and Loula, couldn't come tend to her. I'm feeling kind of poorly myself. But somebody has to stay around here to watch the help, or they would carry off the place inside of an eye blink."

"I don't know much about milling, but if you need a hand, I can spare a few days until Eugenia gets to feeling better and I could use the cash money. That's if you'd have me here abouts. I don't mean to push myself on you if you understand my meaning."

"There isn't much about milling to understand. You unload the bags of grain, weigh them, and write a receipt. Now, your grain is about the best we mill. I can count on yours to be best quality. But some of the others have a lot of chaff mixed into the grain. We have to mill it as whole wheat rather than a fine white flour grade. We ought to sell it as feed. Sometimes there is trash mixed in or dead field mice or, even worse, there is dirt that gives the flour a grit to it. You know what it is like to bite into a pretty buttermilk biscuit and chew on a piece of grit? Lord, there ain't nothing worse than grit. They claim it's my mill stones, but it isn't. My stones are solid granite from way up north in New Hampshire. Them the best there are. Takes more than two months to get a pair down here. And they cost me a small fortune with the shipping cost and all. Yes sir. I could use a hand, if you get all your grain sent in."

"I've got me about two more days of hauling if'n my wagons don't break down. So, I can start with you day after 'morrow, if'n you please. I'd like forty cents a day wages and feed for my mule whilst we are here."

"Done deal." Cyrus stuck out his hand. His shake was as good as his word. A fella could take his word to the bank.

During four month's milling season, the work was long and hard. The machinery set the pace, not the worker. Cyrus wanted to put in gas lights but feared they would spark the milling dust on fire and burn the place down. Then he thought about getting one of those Thomas Edison electric generators and stringing lights in fireproof glass bulbs so the milling could go nonstop all night, but he never followed through with the notion. He mentioned his idea to Bart a time or two, but Bart didn't know about electricity. One walk-through look at the mill works and Bart had the process in his head. There was nothing electric about it. Everything was driven by the flow of the water over the big wheel.

The mill was built over the pond spill of Butler Creek.

Cyrus' daddy had excavated the pond site with a drag line and had poured a Portland-ement dam when times were prosperous. Cyrus was just a toddler when all this happened. Then all his family went off to fight the war with Mexico and didn't come home. The mill had been his since he was a teenager.

Cyrus was no saint except in the eyes of Eugenia. He chewed at a plug of tobacco, took a drink of hard cider to open his lungs, and could be heard cursing when something took a notion to break. He could stand outside of the mill and tell you exactly what was being milled, how many revolutions the stones were moving, and who was at the controls without ever stepping into the building. He knew his business all right. When Eugenia got up from her sick bed, she was just as good as her Pa at feeling the works.

Cyrus was a small man in stature, not weighing in at more than 125 pounds. Bart made up nearly two of him. Seeing the two of them standing side by side, one would think Cyrus was the boy and Bart the man. During his younger years, Cyrus could out-work any man hands-flat-down. He had some age on him now that slowed him down to three-quarter speed. If he didn't keep a hat on his head at all times, you could see that his hair had considerably retreated from his forehead.

Cyrus expressed a desire for Bartholomew to remain at the mill after Eugenia returned. He was given a raise in wages to fifty cents a day or three dollars a week if he worked Saturdays. Without lights, the work days in the winter months were nearly five hours shorter than in the summer months. Bartholomew was concerned about his own farming operation. He knew the wages he was earning at the mill were more than he could make by farming. Since the mill ran from sunrise to sunset, he would have no time remaining for his farming.

He asked Cyrus, "If'n I stay on here and don't get a crop in and then you decide to let me go, I'll be down the creek with no paddle."

"How do you mean?"

"If'n I stays here, I can't be at my farm to do the spring

plowin' and plantin'. Then I won't have a crop to harvest to carry me through the next summer. We gotta look at the long haul of things."

"You could turn your fields to pastures and raise some beef. They don't need much tending. You could look after them morning and night."

"That might be so, but there would be a mess of fencing to get up. I'd need the Saturday and Sunday to get it done 'cause it would take a heap of time to cut and plant them posts. Then I'd need to string and pull wire. That'd be a mess of money that I ain't got."

"How many acres you got cleared?"

"Just 'bout seventy if'n you include the house and outs."

"You got more than enough credits here at the mill for the wire. We can get by with you have gone on weekends except during harvest time."

"So, you talking 'bout six to nine months more work here?"

"I'm talking about forever."

"Um, that's a might long time. I'd have to rethink forever. Then there's the cost of the feeders. I'd be able to put three per acre without crowding them much. So then, I'd be able to hold a couple hundred head. Mind you, I won't start off in a big way, maybe twenty to begin with."

"Beef is bringing a decent price at market. Some better than the grains."

"Maybe, I'll put in a crop of clover and let it seed itself into a pasture. I hear tell beef fatten right quick on clover. I'd have to go a seed huntin'."

"We've got some mail-order catalogues around. I think I could get you good pricing on whatever you might need. And your credits should take care of the cost on that too, but that would be about all that's left. You'd be out of credits."

"So, I could turn to beef farming and use what credits I've saved up?"

"That would be right."

"And you'd guarantee me work until then?"

"Yep."

"Well, alright." They shook their hands to seal the agreement.

"I still got my worries about them beef cattle. They're like children - always need watching and tending. And me be gone all the day. Then there's the cow sickness, bad dogs, black bears, and them poachers with nobody to run them off. I'd be take'un some losses."

"You'd be taking losses even if you were there. Just like that preacher running off with everything right under our noses. Some things can't be helped."

"That's true."

"How did you come by that place anyhow? I'm not trying to be nosey, but I was just wondering."

"Came through my momma's kin. She had two brothers but they was killed off during the Civil War at Cowpens, believe my daddy told me. She weren't my real momma, but that's what I'd call her. She was old and frail. My dad called her Miss. Anna Bell by name. She needed some hands after the darkies ran off, and my daddy took to working her fields. She had a sister living with her with a missing leg. She was mean as a rattler. When they died off, the place was left to my daddy. My real mom died off early. I never knew much of her except for a picture. My daddy took another bride, Ma Kate. They took sick and died. I was all that was left, so I got the place."

"So, you got it by circumlocution?"

"Don't know what that means."

"It was given to you by folk that weren't kin."

"Well, my daddy was."

"But he wasn't kin to the two sisters either."

"No. But he kept them up all their lives."

"How many acres are in the place?"

"Better than two hundred."

"That's a good piece of land, worth a hundred to a hundred and fifty."

"Worth more with the barns and cabin."

"With fencing even more. What do you pay in land taxes?"

"Last year they wanted four dollars and twelve cents. Every year it goes up a few more pennies. If them taxes get much higher, I'll be buying the place back from them on a regular basis."

"It's all the public-work projects to get people back to work."

"I never seen a need to stop working. Never knew nuthing different but work."

"That's what I like about you."

"What's that?"

"You don't mind working. There's a mess of citizens that think the government should be paying them relief."

"Relief from what?"

"Most of the relief is in the big cities where the factories have shut down and let all the workers off. The do-gooders set up soup and bread lines to keep them fed."

"What in tarnation you talkin' 'bout?"

"People aren't buying cars and refrigerators and stoves or houses."

"Lord! What do they need all them things fer?"

"When people buy them, the factories make more. Then the factories need more people to work to make them. They get paid and spend their money to buy what they make."

"Doesn't make a bit of sense to me. I've got all I need."

"You need barbed wire for your cattle. Somebody has to make it and sell it to you. That makes jobs for people so they can spend their wages and profits for the owners to buy more equipment."

"I know what cha talking 'bout now."

"I ain't got no need fer a 'frigerator or car long as I got my spring water and Daisy."

"Well, there you have it. Every time you earn and spend a dollar, it gets spent by others ten more times."

"Why ten?"

"Well by then, your original dollars have been taxed away," Cyrus said.

"And the gov'ment gets it to hire road builders and stuff."

"Exactly right."

"And that dollar gets stuck in a road and not in my pocket?"

"Yes. Now you know all there is to know about commerce and politicians."

"That's a whole heap to think 'bout. You sure shook up my brains with these dollars coming and going. I'll bet you got a mess of dollars stuck in that mill."

"That's why I need it to run all the time. If it stands still, I can't make the dollars work for us they just sit there and waste away."

"Like my fields growin' weeds and scrub and needin' a lot of work to clean 'em up."

"Same but different. The only way this mill is going to make money is to keep running. When the mill makes money, we make money - money for your wages and money to make repairs and pay taxes."

"I don't plan fer my land to waste away. With a little bit of work, it can always be productive."

"And productivity means value. The land will always be worth something. But fencing and cattle make it worth more because a man can make a living off of it. He can support himself and a family."

"Speaking of family, I wonder if I could have your permission to court Eugenia?"

"I'll speak to her about your request. You seem to be an honorable man. You know she wants a man to be a Christian believer."

"Just what does all that mean?"

"You would have to be churched."

"You mean go to Solid Rock on a regular basis?"

"Something like that."

"But I'd need the Sunday for the fencin' and clover plantin' least for another year. Besides, those people don't care a hoot fer me."

"Like I said, I'll talk to her and tell her of your plans and our agreement. I think she would be proud of how you're improving yourself."

"I thank you for your good word on my behalf. Right now, I think this mill needs us a more. I'm a'hearin' something that don't sound right. There may be trash in the slew that needs tending."

Bartholomew waited the remainder of the week for some kind of recognition from Eugenia that Cyrus had spoken to her about their courting.

Cyrus waited until the Sunday after church to speak of the matter when they were seated for dinner.

"I had a conversation with Bart about his staying on permanently."

"Oh? What'd he say?"

"He said he could if he could change over to beef farming. He would have to fence and string wire, and that would take him all of his weekends to get the job done."

"That sounds reasonable."

"He said he would work six days when the milling season is in full swing which might drag out the fencing."

"How much is he going to fence?"

"He said about seventy acres. He's got over two hundred acres on the tax books. I also promised him fifty cents a day."

"That's more than we've paid any hand."

"I think he's going to be worth it. He can practically run the place single handed. He does the work of two of the others. He never stops going."

"You know how some look good until you give them a raise, then they get sorry."

"You talk like he was a horse on sweet feed."

"I think he has a way to go. He's not literate like us. More schooling would do him and us some good. I still do most of the tallies and figuring."

"The two of you work well together. He also asked me about courting."

"Who?"

"You."

Eugenia's face reddened. She cleared her throat. "And?"

"I told him I would talk to you about it. I think he's sweet on you."

Eugenia shifted uneasily in her chair.

"I haven't met a better man. I think he would make a good provider for you and a good son-in-law to me. He does have a good head on his shoulders. But you are right, he could use some polish."

"Polish! He got more rough edges than a rough-cut saw plank."

"That may be true, but I don't want you to spend the rest of your life inside the mill. Your mother needs tending to, and, if you ever want to raise a family, you'll need to stay about the house. I could sell the mill, or you could be a spinster and stay at the mill until you have to sell it."

"What you're saying is that either I marry or you'll sell the mill?"

"Not exactly."

Eugenia burst into tears. Her shoulders and bosoms heaved in spasms. Her napkin covered her face.

"I want to give you your life back. You know I could not have run the mill all these years without you at my side. You've done a man's work better than any other. I'm proud of you and what you've done. I'm just saying that I think Bartholomew can set you free to be a wife and mother without the mill as your daily burden."

Eugenia lifted her tear-soaked eyes and blew her nose free of the sniffled drips. "You've got it all figured out. You've always wanted a son. If that is what you want, then I'll obey your command."

"Command! I've never commanded you. And I'm not

now." Cyrus rose from his seat and placed an arm around Eugenia's shoulder. "I think this is what your mother would wish for you."

"Do you want me to stay home?"

"For heaven's sake, no. Bart has a lot to do, with the farm and all. It would be another year before he or anybody could take your place. The two of you need time to get to know each other. A proper engagement - your mother knows better on these matters - shouldn't be less than a year."

"I'll agree to court him on one condition."

"What's that?"

"You don't sell the mill."

"I'll agree to that. It's yours anyway, darling."

"I think you should tell mother and put it on paper in your will that I will inherit the mill whether I have children or not, and that you will never sell it without having my consent first."

"I'll see the judge in the morning and have him draw the papers just like you said."

"Then it's agreed. I'll court Bartholomew Rombert. You tell him I expect to see him at regular church, bathed, clean shaven, and with new shoes and a pocket handkerchief."

CHAPTER THREE

The Reverend Allston Henslowe kept traveling along through the early winter. He crossed state lines and was deep in the coal country of West Virginia. He stopped along his travels to preach at tent revivals and annual church meetings, any place he could find shelter and a hot meal. He presented himself as a circuit preacher passing the word of the Lord wherever one or two would gather. He helped himself to the offering collection to defray his traveling expenses so he wouldn't have to dig into his larder. He would if he had to.

Henslowe kept the stash of gold coins in a secret compartment under the buggy seat. He had packed the money in a box of sawdust to minimize the clinking sound coins might make if they happened to be jiggled on a bumpy road surface. He constantly worried about the gold when his buggy was out of sight. He worried about the buggy being stolen in the dark of the night. Often, he had frightful dreams of his gold being discovered and being exposed as a fraud and thief. He couldn't help himself when he checked again and again to be sure the box was still in its hiding place. He feared he would be watched and battled with himself to curb his compulsion to check once again.

The winter turned bitterly cold. Mixed with an unusual amount of snow and occasional sleet, his flight had become encumbered by bad weather. Often, he would be taken in by hospitable families until the weather cleared and he could proceed. His clothing would be cleaned and his belly filled with rich home cooking. He took great pleasure in blessing every little morsel, thus endearing the household matron and usurping his patron's hospitality. Often, the food would be only lukewarm when he finished his praise.

The children at his latest respite, Phoebe, Ruth, Clara and Charles, squirmed and fidgeted through his long gospel-quoting orations. Clara Hollenger, youngest daughter of Durk and Myra, had pitifully weak legs. They thought she had contracted the polio because a Doctor Toller had told them so after a brief examination. The Hollengers asked Henslowe to cure her with a miracle of his faith just like Jesus had in Biblical times.

Henslowe responded by saying, "I will need a revelation from God."

"Reverend, do you think we might need to take a fast?"

Thinking of sustaining his portly appetite, "Oh, no. A benevolent Lord would not be pleased for all to suffer in penance for one. I must retire to my quarters and pray. You may favor me with a tray whilst I have a sabbatical retreat."

Henslowe thought about slipping out in the night if the weather weren't so foul and avoid the inevitable confrontation of their disappointment in him. He thought again and remarked to Myra Hollenger at the arrival of his breakfast tray, "A revelation from God might take some time since He has so much on his mind and so many other blessings are being asked. He's very busy, but I'll pray day and night." Thus, he bought a little time for better weather and a few more hot meals.

When Henslowe sold all his pounding from the Solid Rock Primitive Baptist Church, he held back Bartholomew Rombert's amber honey for no other reason than having a penchant for sweets. Although he had not opened the jar, he had anticipated dipping a finger in the viscous amber liquid to satisfy an anticipated craving. Henslowe also had a flask of cider whisky which he sipped from to cut the bone-rattling chill of being exposed in the open carriage. He thought about feeding a teaspoon mixed with a little of the hard cider to Clara as an elixir. He thought it couldn't do the child a bit of harm.

Then, he hatched another plan, wilder than any plan he had ever hatched. He could have a seance and pretend to conjure up the spirit of the evil polio demon. He would put a hex on it. The spirit would beg him to remove the hex. He would do so only if the evil polio spirit removed his poison influence from the child. He could put candles and crosses and Bibles around the table. He could secretly blow on the candles to make the flame flicker then tell them the evil spirit had arrived. The more he thought about the idea, the more excited he got. If he got his act down pat as being a Divine healer, he could name his price. People would give him all their money to heal them and make them well again. He would pack up and be long gone before… he didn't want to think about consequences.

When the next meal tray arrived, he told Myra he needed his healing medication from his buggy. She sent Clara to fetch his black satchel tote it to his room.

He mixed three parts honey to one part cider. Neither flavor overpowered the other. He took a sprig of winter mint and crushed it in a glass. He took the mixture and strained it through his handkerchief and into a saucer. He declared it to be "Perfect!"

He called Durk and Myra and announced, "I have found my revelation. We will have a seance tonight and call the demon spirit of the polio to lift his curse upon Clara. God willing, that is. Place all the crosses, large and small, on the big table with Bibles. A couple of candles are all we need to get started."

They did exactly as he bade of them. "Everything is in readiness, just like you asked."

"Then assemble the family around the table," the reverend ordered. "I will be down shortly."

When he arrived, they waited for his further instructions.

"Place Clara on the table dressed only with her night-gown. I will anoint her with an elixir as I pray." Henslowe sat at her side and placed the bowl at her head.

"What about the other children? Can we do it without them?" Myra asked.

"We would need Clara, but the others can be dismissed if you wish. They will need to leave the room and be very quiet."

"Okay, you heard him." Myra said to the children. "Phoebe, Ruth, and Charles, go to our bedroom. Get on your knees and pray silently. I'll come and get you when we are done. Don't you be afeard none, we ain't going no whares."

Henslowe continued, "Each of you must hold Clara's hands and close your eyes tightly. Roll them back like you are going to sleep. Concentrate on seeing the demon pox spirit burning in hell. Picture the flames in your mind. Once you are relaxed, take a deep breath and let it out slowly. That way I'll know you are ready to begin."

"Is everybody ready now?" Henslowe somberly asked. He unbuttoned his vest for easier breathing. His belly sagged onto his lap.

The remaining heads nodded. "As you concentrate on the candle flames on the table, I want you to think of the healing power of the elixir and how much good it will do Clara to make her whole again and make her legs normal like her brother and sisters and any other child not so inflicted with the poison. I want you to let out that deep breath slowly and totally relax as I summon the evil polio spirit and put a hex upon him for deforming this precious little child of God. I want you to think about the evil spirit he has put in her rising like steam from her body. I want you to pray that I can put a hex on him if he don't make her well and leave her alone."

Henslowe's hand slid under Clara's gown and up toward her immature bosom. He toyed with her nipples until they were firmly hardened and erect. He was having one himself. He kept thinking, "This is God's will." His hand slid down from her breasts, slowly down her abdomen, plummeted a finger into her navel, past and lower still until upon the juncture of her legs. She stiffened herself by pressing her knees together tightly. She tightened her grip with Myra and Durk as Henslowe's finger penetrated her privacy. Her young face winced in agony. She gasped, then moaned with a whining sigh. He raptured in her agony.

He pulled his hand quickly away in fear someone would open their eyes and catch him fondling her pubescence. He realized he had the right to put his hand anywhere he wished; it was God's will that she should be cleansed with his ointment. Anyone would only believe his hand under her gown was part and parcel of a well-intended good deed. Clara was too inexperienced to know that she was being raped by his hand.

"Close your eyes ever more tightly," Henslowe began. "In your mind's eye, relax all of your body and embrace the Almighty." The pious reverend dipped his fingers in the liquid and slid them under her gown, groping into Clara again, vigorously. She opened her legs slightly and began to find pleasure where there had been fear.

"In the name of the Lord God Almighty, I ask that the elixir be the cure and that Clara take the saucer in both hands now knowing that every last drop is for her salvation and purification from the polio evil. Clara, I command you to lick every last drop from the saucer so that none remains, not even a scent of what was once on the saucer. Clara, the Lord God Almighty commands that you will feel a tingling in your mouth. That sensation will spread down your throat all over your body and bring the healing to your legs. Clara, Grip your parents' hands once again. You will feel the tingling coming from the hand of your mother, Myra, and from the hand of your father, Durk, who first gave you life and who now give you life anew. For this is the wish and blessing of the Lord God Almighty that the polio evil will leave you forever."

Allston Henslowe blew out the candles and so loudly exclaimed "Hallelujah" as to cause Myra and Durk to jolt.

When Durk stuck a match to reignite the smoldering candles, the reverend was slumped in his chair exhausted from the charade. His erection had been whipped supple.

Clara was carried to bed and tucked in with a kiss. "Will I get better now?" she asked.

"I hope so. I could feel the tingling in my hand. Could you?"

"I think so. I felt it in my wee-wee especially."

"Oh, that's wonderful. How did the stuff in the saucer

taste?" Myra asked.

"I don't know how to describe it. Sweet, then hot, then minty. I could feel it go all the way down my gullet."

"Sleep tight. Call me if you need anything."

Durk thanked the Reverend Henslowe for the healing. Myra, who was not given to a display of emotion, fought back tears when she returned to the table. She could not speak. Her chin quivered as she picked up the crosses and Bible. She fell back into her chair and buried her face in her arms.

Henslowe and Durk looked at one another, then back to her. "Are you all right, darling?" Durk asked.

Myra lifted her head and said, "Reverend Henslowe, I felt the presence of the Lord in this room tonight, placing her hand upon his. I know Clara will walk. Thank you for all that you have done. You have given us a blessing."

"Yes sir." Durk said, "I felt the same tingling in my spirit. But the missus has a better way with words. I just want you to know you can stay with us as long as you desire."

Henslowe's tingling sensations were of a different sort. He buttoned his vest. "You folk have been very kind to me and my tribulations. Your kindness is much appreciated, and I accept your invitation until the weather clears and a man can travel without fear from the elements."

Henslowe stayed several months, continuing the therapeutic massages to Clara and himself in the special healing places. Clara thought he had control of the devil who kept her from walking normally. She wanted to please her parents. In spite of her initial reluctance, she let him have his way with her even to the point of removing her gown and under garments privately in the seclusion of the tiny bedroom. He stayed and ate huge portions with a generous appetite. He slept late in the day, long after the weather cleared. The yard daffodils and jonquils pushed up yellow and white blooms.

He saw Clara stand on her legs with considerable wobble. Gradually, she took baby steps with the aid of a chair or bed rail or the arm of a family member. Henslowe was as much amazed as the Hollengers were thankful. By the middle of March, she was getting around without much assistance. She tired easily, but by golly she was walking. The private massages became less frequent.

The Hollengers pronounced that the Reverend Allston Henslowe had performed a miracle on their daughter, Clara. Thankfully, the weather had been so foul, the news did not travel farther than a village away. Since electricity has not found a reasonable return on a rural investment, radio broadcasts were absent. Most all news was given and taken at Sunday churching. With warm clear weather in abundance, people gathered to celebrate the Spring, plow, and get seed into the soil in the never-ending ritual of survival.

The word of his healing was spreading. His anxiety increased in proportion to his taste for greed and lust. Others in the community came to Henslowe and asked for healing. He mixed up batch after batch of his miracle elixir and was able to get the price bid up to five dollars in gold coin. Each batch, he swore was to be the last before he moved on.

He would put his hand on the individual, "I declare in the name of the Lord God Almighty, if you drink every last drop of this potion and pray on your hands and knees like a child with all your heart, you will be healed." And they were. Every last one of them was cured of whatever ailed them. Henslowe was getting rich and famous beyond the next village.

One farmer had bought some of the elixir and had fed it to his dry utter cow. The animal quickly recovered and gave more butterfat milk than ever. The word spread. "It could heal sick stock and make them better than new." Henslowe thought, "There is more stock inhabiting the countryside than there are people."

Being famous was among his greatest fears. His lies and thefts at Solid Rock Primitive Baptist Church on the Old Plank Road near Davisville over by Big Top Mountain were haunting him. They were the subject of every whisper, behind every tree. He feared that sooner or later somebody would make the connection and point a finger at him. They would put him right for what he had done. His kind of bad news travels as fast as the good news of a faith healer. He needed to move on into the Ohio Valley area, maybe further west. With the money he had accumulated from selling his elixir, he could buy a homestead, get himself a squaw or free Negro and live like a squire. He might even change his name and build himself a church. He was already thinking of a name for it.

While refilling his bowl of stew, Phoebe whispered, "I need to see you."

Henslowe finished his second helping of bread pudding and excused himself to tend to his horse which was stabled in the Hollengers' barn. He threw a quick wink at Phoebe.

"Reverend Henslowe, I'd be mighty honored if you let me tend to your animal for you."

"Don't be foolish, girl. A man should do his own work," he responded. "Besides you have to clean the table."

"I cleared last night. It's Ruth's turn. I could hold the lantern for you."

Durk said, "That's Charles' job."

"We traded off," Phoebe coyishly responded. Charles was elated that he wouldn't have to go out in the cold.

"All right," Henslowe agreed. "Get your wrap and come along."

The Reverend Allston Henslowe had been taking a little more than just a bed and meals from his kind hosts. He had been sneaking out with Phoebe to the barn on the pretense of tending to his horse on many occasions. He was having his way with her as well. "His will be done," he cooed from his lecherous embrace. Phoebe was bent over the feeding trough. She had seen the farm animals do it that way.

She had just turned sixteen when she whispered that night, "I'm expecting."

"For Christ's sake, child, stop speaking in riddles. Say what you mean."

"I've missed two purges. Won't be long before my mother

knows about the baby growing in my stomach."

"Baby! Gracious Lord! Are you trying to tell me you're pregnant?"

"That's what I mean to say. You have to take me with you."

"Absolutely not! It's out of the question."

"They'll put me out, and I have no wheres to go. You have to."

"I'll consider it. You go back to the house and rest easily. I'll have your answer in the morning."

She heard him move about and sneak out of the house. She heard the noise of the horse and buggy disappear into the night. Anticipating her punishment, tears flooded her face. She had lost hope of ever being able to leave the destitute life of poverty. Henslowe was the only man that had showed an interest in her. She wanted to get away from the remote farm life as much as the Reverend lusted for gold. She pulled up the small window and tried to call him back but could not scream for fear of waking her siblings and parents. She cried in fear of what would become of her.

Henslowe muttered to himself quietly as he led the horse by the reins. When he had put sufficient distance between himself and the Hollengers, he boarded the buggy. Brilliant moonlight illuminated the roadway, making his escape easy. The stars sparkled like salt sprinkled on a navy blanket. There were no clouds above or in his mind. He continued his muttering until he had thoroughly absolved himself and thoroughly damned Phoebe to eternal Hell for her sinful behavior. He never looked back. Henslowe only had one vial of his watered-down potion remaining in his coat pocket. He needed more.

By the middle of the next day, Henslowe put better than twenty miles between himself and the Hollengers. He knew people had made a pilgrimage of more than that distance on the rumors of his healing. He kept going through the night into the mid-morning until he was sure he had outrun his reputation before he stopped for refreshment at the Wayside Colonial Inn. His horse was wasted from the exhausting journey.

He ordered a meat pie of mutton and some beer. He requested a package of food and refreshment to take with him. He requested a feed bag be given to his horse.

A scrawny man with a red bandana knotted on his head seated at a dark corner table studied Henslowe. He received an inconspicuous nod from the barkeeper. He silently left the establishment and waited for Henslowe to come out. He gave the horse a feed bag of oats.

"Where you heading?" the innkeeper's wife asked.

"Nowheres special. Thought I would travel till I felt comfortable with where I found myself."

"Where'd you come from?"

"Been traveling around on the preaching circuit doing as the good Lord asked of me."

"So, you're a man of the cloth? You're not dressed like a parson?"

"I'm a Baptizer of men like John in the Bible."

"Oh. That will be a twenty-cent piece for the food and drink."

"All I've got on me is fifteen cents. Will that do?"

"Might have to take the package back." Looking toward her husband, the barkeeper, "Randall? This here man says he's a preacher and wants to short you five cents. What d' you think?"

The barkeep looked in Henslowe's direction and said, "Let's hear him do some preachin' for his vittles."

"I'll need to get my Bible from the buggy."

"Fella, you ain't going no damn place." The barkeeper was the size of two of Henslowe and had scars on his head and face. His hands were as big as dinner plates.

"You want me to crack your scrawny little fly neck with a flick of my finger?"

"No. Let me check my pockets. I might have a few more coins. Times are hard, and money isn't easy to come by. Here are a couple of two-cent pieces. I'm only a penny short now. You let me go on my way, and I'll bless you for the next hour. I swear."

"Listen to that. A swearing preacher. Now, don't that just about beat all. Ha! Ha! Get yourself out of here, and I never want to see your cheatin' eyes again. You hear me preacher man?"

"Yes, sir. Thank you." Henslowe snatched his package and scuffled out the door.

"How 'bout givin' me a ride up the road a piece there, preacher," the bandana-clad man spoke sharply as he untied the horse's feed bag.

The voice startled Henslowe, "What?"

"This here road can be mighty treacherous for somebody that don't know their way here 'bouts." The man jumped into the buggy without agreement.

"I'm not sure I need company."

"There are marauders and highwaymen waiting to ambush and hijack all about these parts. The woods are full of thieves and killers too. You best be advised to accept my company."

"Only till the next crossroads. Then I must insist you get out and find your own way. God will be my Shepherd," Henslowe insisted.

After they had rounded the first bend in the road, the companion hit Henslowe on the back of the head with a billet. The hitchhiker rifled Henslowe's pockets and baggage for plunder. All he found was a silver cross and the diluted-down vial of Bartholomew's miraculous honey. Disappointed, the robber tossed it on the ground beside the buggy and fled. He kept the silver cross.

When Allston revived, his bruised head thunderously ached. He wiped the blood from the knot growing on the back of his head. He righted himself in the buggy. Feeling faint, he swooned from the buggy onto the ground. His hand fell on top of the discarded vial. He pulled the stopper and completely drained the potion. Within minutes, he felt revitalized. He felt as though years of hard living had been swept away from his body. His aching head went away. His stiff back from being in the buggy all both nights and half the day was evaporated.

"I'll be darn!" he exclaimed. "This stuff really works."

He lay on the ground feeling a full measure of bliss. He exclaimed of his abundant life. He felt joy in the puffy-white clouds above the budding trees. He could smell the flowers and hear the magnificent sounds of nature as though they were an orchestra playing his favorite melody. He wanted to dance and sing and celebrate. He was euphoric for the first time in his life.

"The honey!" he thought. "It's the honey from the church. There's something about that honey that is like nothing else in the world. If I had half-good sense, I would go back to Davisville and get the whole hive." A moment later as he jumped into the buggy, he said, "I think that's what I'll do."

Henslowe took off with a jolt, whipping the devil out of the old horse till welts swelled on her rump and she was lathered about the mouth. He arrived at a crossroads that would take him east. From there, he was able to reckon a route to circumvent Hollenger country by a wide margin. He figured a week's good travel would get him close to his honey.

In the meantime, he had to figure a story of why he had hastily departed with the Solid Rock Primitive Baptist Church's money. He would have to surrender their gold to make an amends, to win their favor. He figured the act would be an easy trade since he had made thirty times the sum from bogus peddling of Bartholomew's honey. The church's few coins were insignificant in comparison to the thousands he could extort when he possessed the entire hive. That which he would gain was far greater than that which he would have to forfeit. Mentally, he measured the stacks of gold - always gold, never silver or copper coins. For Henslowe, only gold had the exciting smell and glitter to satiate his craving.

CHAPTER FOUR

Elmer County split from Washington County at the beginning of the Civil War conflict. The Washington Country politicians supported the Confederacy, while supporters of Jason Elmer did not. Generally speaking, one county had slaves, and the other did not. There were grey lines in places, but one tolerated the other with a decency of mutual distrust. Both sides of the split county sent men to fight for the southern cause of state rights.

Both sides knew the real issue centered on the Republican party's desire to capture the votes of the emancipated slaves to guarantee themselves as the power brokers of American politics. To acquire the loyalty of the coveted black vote, the Republicans could not allow the southern confederacy to stand independent. Often calling themselves Dixiecrats, the South had always voted solidly Democrat. They had controlled the national government long before the Republicans were swept into power over the morality issue of slavery.

In any event, as things would have their way, part of the Republican payoff for loyalty was that Elmer County got an Electric Membership Corporation, funded by the Federal government, and Washington Country didn't. Lines were strung on poles everywhere, even to Palmer's Dry Goods store where Bart Rombert saw his first electric light on the day the switch was turned. He was one of about fifty people including Eugenia and Cyrus who had gathered for the celebration. The power from the plant came down the line in the middle of the day. Nobody really noticed a big difference between the sunlight and the illumination from the single glass bulb. It just glowed with a yellow-orange tint and got hot to the touch.

"Well, if that's all there's to 'lectricity, then it don't matter all that much," said one.

"What's the big deal?" asked one.

"So, this is what the fuss is all about," said another.

"If'n God wanted us to have 'lectricity, he would'a made the sun to burn all day and all night."

"Ain't nearly as bright as a coal lantern."

"How much you pay fer that wired candle?"

"Can't blow that 'un out."

"Ain't got no smell to it."

Every person had a comment and a rebuttal to a comment and a comment to render on the comment. They carried on for the best part of an hour. Some were awestricken as though they had seen a miracle, while others joked at the foolishness of making a big to do about nothing. Some left to tell others about what they saw. New spectators arrived. Seth Palmer left his light on all night. Horses and riders came and went. Buggies and wagons stopped for a view. Even Cedric Oliver and his family arrived in their Studebaker motor car for a look see. The bulb was the attraction for several more weeks until people sort of got used to it and forgot about the novelty. Every now and again, a customer at Palmer's would ask Seth to turn the light on. The customer would gasp and walk all around it and stare until a temporary spot would appear on everything in the store the customer looked at. The afterglow always brought additional comments.

"Damn thing has ruined my eyesight."

"It 'un burned a hole in my eye."

"My eyes are going to be sore for a week now."

"How can you stay in here with that glass bulb a staring at you'un all the day long?"

"Does that thing give you a flesh burn?"

The other merchants, across the street and on both sides of Palmer, called a meeting down at the church and decided to look into having lights strung along the main street. A collection was taken by the town folk to get a pool going for what they thought would be the cost. The county chipped in for the extra wires. Terry's Lumber Company put up the poles with convict labor from the jail house. Folks declared that the town needed a proper name and a post office. Palmer, who attended the meeting, was elected by the other merchants as mayor. The others, including Cyrus Boyd, called themselves councilmen. They agreed to serve a term of two years without compensation. They organized a merchants' society and collected fifty cents-a-year dues and named the little hamlet "Rockville" after the closest church.

After they erected a "Welcome to Rockville" sign on the road leading into and out of the cluster of small shacks, somebody got to thinking there weren't any rocks around and foreigners might expect to find rocks for sale. Another council meeting was held to consider the thought. Of course, the meeting was announced at the church for the following Wednesday. "Anybody that might have a name for the town should come." Someone remembered, "The great battles of the Civil War were named after a river if'n there weren't no town close by." So, they came up with the name "Butler" because of the nearby creek that fed the pond at Cyrus Boyd's mill. Nobody would mistake "Butler" for a rock.

Ellis Summer decided to open a bar next to the livery stable so liquor could be bought by the glass. This caused a big fuss among the women folk in general and the churchgoers in specific. Ellis didn't last long in the business when the county chairman, Donald Asbury, told him over a glass of Canadian rye whiskey that any such establishment as his needed a permit from the county, and he doubted one could be issued for the sale of spirits. For a few dollars every so often, he could cool off the wasps that were flying about as to let him get his investment money back.

Good to his word, Asbury spoke to the ladies of the church within the week. He told them in a fiery speech "alke-hol was not permitted in the country" and he'd "have Mister Ellis Summer's establishment boarded up and him run out of town right soon." There was heated debate by some on the subject since the county did not vote favorably on the constitutional amendment in the first place. "Them damn Yankees have trampled on our rights long enough," somebody shouted. Cedric vehemently took offense in having the word "damn" attached as a prefix to the word "Yankee."

Hearing Asbury make all the promises seemed to pacify them women folk. Most all the men folk knew they could get decent shine from Donald Asbury anyhow. Having him watch over things just made them feel all the better. Summer's bar was a lot more convenient for some than traveling way up to the courthouse to have Asbury pull jars from his trunk.

Once electricity came into Butler, it wasn't long before a telephone wire was hung on all the same poles. Always ahead of his time, Palmer mounted a telephone box on the wall of his store and took messages from the out-of-town kin when there was news like a death in the family and such all. Everybody stopped talking when the phone rang. Only Seth was allowed to answer the summons.

Seth Palmer got the post office contract. He boxed a cage in the corner to the right of his front door as the official Butler Branch of the United States Post Office. He hung a two-lined sign: "Post cards one Cent, letters two Cents." A cabinet maker built a three-by-four-foot box of pigeonholes for mailbox subscribers. Seth set it on a counter in his post office. Stamps were sold, and parcel post packages from mail order catalogs were received. Most folk came and got their mail, mostly on Saturday, the milling day. If mail stayed at Palmer's over a month and the addressee did not have a box, Norma Harrington contracted to make home deliveries. The recipient usually gave her a gratuity, not always money, for her effort.

Palmer got so busy in his place he had to split his merchandising plumb in half. The feed and seed and farm implements went down the street a stretch, and all the other dry goods stayed where they were. Splitting the business was the best idea Palmer ever thought up. A man could go into the feed and seed and sit all day by the stove playing checkers and telling stories and not be bothered by the female gossip. Men could talk about the weather and the bugs and politics and other such stuff as was important. A man could chew and spit without having to go outside. There wasn't a telephone ringing or someone yelling into the horn. Best of all, a man could scratch, burp, and blow gas without having to look about and say "Excuse me."

A feller named Aaron Cohen acquired a piece of town land and built Butler's first brick building. Cohen took twice as long to put it up - all two floors, as it takes to put up a stick-built building of the same proportion. The bottom floor was walled down the middle. He and his missus planned to live above. The bricks had to be special hauled in from way past Davisville in a big freight wagon. He didn't use a single creek stone, not even in the foundation. His building was the first not built on rock pilings as underpins. The bricks went right into the ground and all around like a government building. It must have cost him a fortune.

Mr. Cohen opened up a ready-made clothing shop for men, women, and children. He sold everything you could put on your body including ladies' jewelry and timepieces. He had oriental carpets on his floors and thick drapes in the windows. On the other side of his building, he got a bank started which he named the Elmer National Bank. He had a big safe box cemented right into the wall with a combination lock and a timer mechanism. He made mortgages and lent money. You could take your money to him, and he would pay 2-percent interest just to hold it safe. He went back and forth from one side to the other. He always put on a round domed, English-style hat and a fine coat, rain or shine, when making the short trip. He was peculiar that way.

The Cohens brought living to be something nobody, except folks at the courthouse, knew about. He had inside plumbing and toilets. When he got his electricity, he pumped water from the well to a roof tank. When they turned the spigot, they'd get water that had been heated by the sun. They also had a refrigerator that made ice even in the summertime. Why, when you'd go in there to buy a pair of winter wool socks, Miss Stella'd bring you a glass of sweet tea with ice cubes in it. After a natural while, he'd let you use his "Crapper" toilet. You could rinse your hands in hot water from the bathroom lavatory. They had many customers who would buy some insignificant item just to experience the marvel of indoor flush plumbing and hot water from a spigot.

He was a fine gentleman and did a really good business from customers coming from all over. Stella was, by a far measure, the best dressed woman in the county. There was some talk about him being the next mayor of Butler.

None of the prosperity in the town of Butler was lost on Cyrus, Eugenia, and Bartholomew. They inspected every wire, breaker box, bulb, insulator, switch and motor that electricity flowed through in the town that might make something work, including the Cohen's refrigerator. Bart swore at how complicated all the new electric inventions were making life. On the other hand, he was figuring in his mind every place in the mill where the electric energy might be used to cut cost or increase productivity. Cyrus and Eugenia were doing the same.

The water from the pond cost nothing to turn the wheel. The energy was directly converted from the wheel shaft to a bevel gear. This was where the first break in motion was located. The bevel gear could be engaged or disengaged as needed. The water could also be diverted from the wheel in the event repairs were necessary. Everything else in the mill that moved was driven by a main overhead shaft onto which leather belts were looped. Cyrus had three sets of millers in a row, wheat, corn and cracked feed. The wheat had the best quality and newest set of thousand-pound stones.

All three agreed to Cyrus' original plan. String light inside and put on a second shift. The cost would be paid by the profits from the additional milling charges. Bart pointed out that they should ponder the purchase of a motorized truck to pick up the grain from farmers and to deliver the flour to warehouses and merchants in Davisville. The reason being, he said, "We can mill more flour and grist more corn than we could sell here 'bouts. With so much piled up everywhere, we'd have to drop our price down to shake ourselves loose of it."

Eugenia added, "That's true. Why not take it to market? We already got the best price anywhere around. We can get some of those imprint cotton bags rather than burlap sacks and call our flour something like 'Snow White Flour.'"

Cyrus said, "We'd have to buy a new bagger to keep up."

"It's just that I think we need to get with the times, Pa. We need to get modern. This is 1923. We could still sell it in five-pound flour sacks for the local folks, until we sell more wholesale that retail."

"The two of you have a real good head for business. Whatever you think is best is what we will do then. I don't want to get too big too fast. We can't spend money faster than we make it."

A letter was received at Palmer's addressed to the members of The Solid Rock Primitive Baptist Church. There was nothing more than "Reverend Allston Henslowe" for a return address. The postage was cancelled in Bismark, Tennessee. No one had heard of the place but assumed it to be way up the Appalachian mountains. Seth Palmer held the letter until Cyrus Boyd and Ed Watson were in the store then he opened the letter and read it out loud. His dark bushy eyebrows twitched above his glasses with every word he spoke.

"Greetings, my dear members of Solid Rock Primitive Baptist Church. I hope this letter finds you well and in good spirit.

Duty called upon me to attend urgent matters concerning my dear mother in West Virginia, which forbade notice of my abrupt departure. For this, I humbly beg your forgiveness. I found myself in possession of all the church's worldly funds and have been a diligent fiduciary. I would have sent the funds to you by courier but knew of none to trust with such a charge but myself.

God willing, I anticipate my return to you kind people within a fortnight.

Please forgive my delay in correspondence. You have always been in my thoughts and prayers.

In the name of the Lord Jesus Christ,

Allston Henslowe"

"So, that's what happened to the Reverend. I always wondered what came of him," Cyrus exclaimed.

"Everyone will be elated to hear he's coming back with the church's money. Um, um, the things they said about him. Now, won't they be ashamed when they see him roll the coins on the altar," Seth said.

"Seth, you might wanta post that thar letter 'un the front of that thar postal winder fer ever'un to see. I'll pass the words along as I best 'collect to dem I'd see," Ed Watson said.

Cyrus remarked, "That letter will be the talk of the town. Thanks for sharing it with us, Seth."

"Sure takin' his ever-loving time about it," Ed said.

Allston Henslowe was cheating and swindling his way back to the town of Butler. He searched around Harristown in eastern Tennessee where he was preaching to trade his buggy and horse for a motor car. He figured he could make better time than having to stop so often to buy feed and rest his horse. Besides, the buggy was slap worn out. The wood-spoked wheels wobbled off center on the axle giving him a ride with a constant jolt on every rotation. He preached and prayed with those who came to him for spiritual enrichment. He took them to the Tellico River and submerged them in the murky cool water in the name of John the Baptist, all the while talking about his need for motorized transportation.

The people were so impressed with his zeal and fervor for the word of the Lord, they went and got him a 1917 Model-T Ford with a gasoline engine on the condition he would stay on regular and be their preacher man. They went to work setting him up in a thrashing barn and built rows of benches to hold better than fifty people, babies not included. This would be the beginning of the church they had always wanted and the preacher they had needed. God had answered their prayers when He sent Henslowe to them. There was not a moment that went by that someone didn't ask the Reverend Allston, "What can I get fer you?" or "What cha need'n Mister Preacher man?"

Life would have been carefree if it weren't for his lusting for the honey and what it could do for him. What those good people offered was a pittance in comparison to what he planned to get for himself and the life he would live. He had dreams, big dreams, bigger than anyone could imagine.

After he got used to the operation of the gasoline buggy, he took off. He circumvented towns, villages, and hamlets in the Model-T Ford where he might be known and held revivals where he was sure he wasn't. He would stop in a small town and put up posters calling for all Christians to renew their faith. He would weasel himself an invitation, as a circuit-riding preacher, at some local ministry and hold a service on the grounds in the afternoon and a purging in the evening at a creek. Hellfire-and-damnation was his message for all sinners bound for purgatory. Those who put their faith in his word would cough up coins, often at the urging of their wives, as penitence for their wrongful lusting for the seven deadly sins. Allston was most familiar with the sins because he had violated them all, as often as he could.

He kept thinking about the miraculous cures he had made with the honey and wished he had more. He swore he would find the source of the honey and it would be all his. He swore that with the honey, he would be rich and famous beyond his imagination. Nothing and nobody could stop him.

He visualized himself sitting on the veranda attached to a

huge white-marble house overlooking spectacular beds of exotic flowers. There would be fountains of water splashing into tile pools and obscene statues dotting the manicured yard. The estate would have to be in a big city, maybe New York or Washington. The house would be furnished with exquisite antiques collected from all over Europe and the Middle East during extensive tours of his healing enterprise. He would eat from gold plates with a gold fork. He would drink from a gold chalice studded with precious stones. He would have a heated indoor swimming pool like an ancient Roman spa. His servants would bathe him in a large black marble tub filled with heated water and perfumed salts while he sipped imported champagne from a crystal glass. When finished, they would oil him and slip him into a fine robe.

He could see throngs of worshipers falling at his feet in humble reverence. Kings and heads of state would seek private audiences with him. Even the Pope would come to him with a petition for a private moment. He would wear a gold ring with a five-carat diamond that people could kiss if he would grant them the familiarity of closeness. Carpets would be rolled before him so his feet would never touch the ground. A servant would shade him with an umbrella when outdoors and fan him with feathers when reclining.

He visualized himself on his yacht with vivacious servants begging to please his every desire. Any craving would be instantly satisfied no matter how perverse. They would take him in any direction he pointed. When he reached a port, a magnificent carriage would whisk him away to a private villa overlooking the Mediterranean Sea or to a castle overlooking the Rhine or Danube Rivers.

Occasionally, he would jolt back into reality when the secondhand Ford hit a road rock. He could taste the champagne and chocolates, and he could smell the flowers on the veranda and the perfumed salts in his bath water. He could feel the maidens touching his body, arousing his manly instincts. They were fighting among themselves for the right to be with him. Oh, they were such an annoyance when he didn't want them around.

Yes, there were ghouls, dragons, and demons fighting in his head. He wanted peace from the ripping apart of his sanity. They were tearing at his soul. They made him do things that he feared and regretted later. He was not that man doing those things. It was someone else. Like Phoebe, they were evil and corrupt. Not him. The "He" and the "I" were separated into two personalities that were being directed by things beyond the ability of his will to control. He wanted his freedom from them. He wanted a way out from the horrible life that was tearing him apart piece by piece. At times he wanted to hide from himself; other times he wished to be punished for things that he had done to others willingly, in the name of God, without remorse or restrained consciousness of guilt.

He couldn't believe his dream had not yet come true. He pushed the Ford faster and faster to his destination thinking of the honey. Oh, the honey would give him the freedom from his prayers. It was the only way he could save himself from the forces that controlled him and made him do all those bad things.

When he preached his hellfire-and-damnation, he was preaching to himself. He would fall on his knees and beg forgiveness. He would bawl like a child. The congregations and tent followers would think him to be sincerely prostrating himself for their salvation and redemption into the faith of the Lord. No. It was for himself. His own spiritual battle was being played out on the stage before them. Oh yes, it was moving to witness. They gave him money for his suffering, thinking it was their own words of guilt he spoke.

When finished, he felt exhausted as though the good side of him had won the battle. Then temptation would silently creep back into his mind, slowly taking over control. And the evil would awaken and direct him in horrible ways. Soon, he would lie, cheat, steal, and philander with the girls. He couldn't help himself. He couldn't hold himself back from the powerful forces. Again, on the following night, he would punish himself at the podium, on the floor among the very same innocent people that he would be hurting in the twilight hours when he couldn't sleep.

Sleep was what he feared the most. Once, when he awoke, the window curtains, fluttered by the breeze and cast a dancing moonlight shadow on the wall at the foot of his bed. He screamed, fearing it was the devil in the room with him about to take another bite of his soul. He leaped from his bed and fell to his knees, clasping his hands in earnest prayer.

"Our Lord God, don't let this demon-devil grip me in his claws. Save me. I'm worthy of your redemption. I have been a sinner all my wicked life and wish to confess at this final hour. I have stolen; I have fornicated; I have envied another man's wealth; I have coveted property. I'm but a small vessel begging to be filled with the waters of your spirit to do what is right. Oh, please spare me this night. Give me comfort. Give peace and the strength to be your savior on earth as you are in Heaven."

He recited the Lord's prayer and the 23rd Psalm. He prayed finally for the devil to take all of him rather than take one bite of his soul at a time. His torment was tremendous. He prayed for death to overwhelm him. His soul seemed whole again. The devil was cast out. He had strength to resist his temptations. He prayed to be strong and fearless. He prayed for the courage of a hundred men. He prayed to have the honey. The nectar was stronger than the devil, stronger than the will of the Lord God Almighty on his pitiful mortal soul.

When he finally arrived at the Solid Rock Primitive Baptist Church on Sunday morning, everybody that counted was there to hear his explanation and to see their money laid out before them.

"For the Lord is my witness, and he can strike me dead right here at this spot before you, I never intended to take the funds of this fine house of God as my own. There may be assembled here some who may think otherwise and wish to condemn me for having done so. They may be sitting next to you or in front or behind. The shame is their own for first thinking bad thoughts when good intentions were meant. I can tell you there is your money, every last cent of it and that should speak for itself. A man's action is his binding word in the eyes of the Lord and that shall set him free."

Henslowe continued, "Having the money in my possession of this great institution of God has tormented me beyond your belief. I asked myself, 'What if I should be robbed by a highwayman and his ill-gotten money, your money, was taken and used in a sinful way?' In fact, I was accosted by a heathen whose ambition was to snuff out my life. He left me for dead along the road and stole all my worldly possessions. I walked through the shadow of death, and evil was all about me. Your money, all the while, was hidden in a safe place in the carriage. The good Lord watched over me and protected me so that your money could be safely returned to where it rightfully belongs. My firm and true belief held me safe in my journey. I wasn't alone. Your prayers to the Almighty gave me safe return. Yes, brothers and sisters, your faith in the goodness of my soul was my shield in the moment of my despair. You were my rod and staff of encouragement. When I needed you, you were there for me in spirit, and I'm now here in the flesh for you."

Henslowe continued once again, "My dear friends, I regret to report, my good mother has passed to her great reward in heaven. I was by her side as she took her last breath and whispered her last words praising me as her good son that did the bidding of the Lord. The pain of her loss will always be with me and cannot be shared with another. Only those who have experienced great misery, who have lost a loved one, who have traveled the path and stumbled on the stones and pits, can feel the great void which she left in my life. God fills that void with his love."

Henslowe concluded, "I can feel your love, and it swells my heart and keeps the beat regular. Where there was sorrow, there is joy. Where there was pain, there is now love. I hear the resounding gong. I hear the clashing cymbals reverberating from where there was silence and doubt. My dear friends, it is written that 'love is patient, love is kind, it is not jealous, is not pompous, it is not inflated, it is not rude, it does not seek its own interest.' My friends, I thank you for the passion of your love and many other blessings. Amen"

The sweat was pouring off the Reverend Henslowe and dripping onto the floor. His face cloth was saturated. He could have extemporaneously preached for another hour or so, quoting numerous Bible verses from memory as he had often done when he got himself wound up in the spirit. He could put on a show by strutting about, banging his fist on the lectern, shouting and waving his arms like an angry angel attempting to lift off the earth, disgusted with mankind. But on this occasion, he feared someone from the congregation would throw an egg at him or worse, a stone. He feared pockets were full of stones to be heaved at him. He thought that somehow they could see into his evil heart and knew all he said was an attempt to conceal his ambition to find the honey and steal it.

"Let us now raise our voices in singing hymn number 21, 'Blessed Assurance.'"

After the benediction, he stood at the door and waited. He was astonished when people pressed coins in his hand and patted his back. He thanked each for the pounding and questioned a few on the source of the honey. Bartholomew Rombert was not among those attending his forgiveness sermon, but Cyrus and Eugenia were.

"Reverend Henslowe, that was one of the most moving sermons I've ever heard. It brought tears to my eyes as I thought about my dear mother suffering her weakness and what life would be like without her," Eugenia said.

"Oh, my darling child, I will pray for your mother's health and happiness. And you, Mr. Boyd, it seems my brief absence has brought you prosperity. This village is full of bustle."

"You've got to get with the times, they say."

"I also want to thank you for the pounding. What was it you brought? I just can't remember right off."

"We brought black-walnut pound cake. And Bartholomew Rombert brought you a jar of his honey," Eugenia answered.

"Oh, do say. And where is that fine young man today? I would like to thank him personally."

"He's gone off to see about a delivery truck. You can find him at the mill early next morning if you like."

"Thank you, and God blesses him and the Boyds."

Allston Henslowe's wheels were spinning. He now knew who brought the honey, but not where the hive could be found. Monday morning, first thing, he would pry out Mr. Rombert. He would have his honey that very day and be gone from this place.

CHAPTER FIVE

The basic beehive is an assembly of two boxes separated by a screen wire. The wire prevents the queen bee from depositing her eggs in the upper box, or super. Since the queen is much larger than the workers and drone bees, she can't squeeze through the screen. So, she lays her eggs exclusively in the bottom box, aptly called the brood chamber. Hence, when robbing a hive of the precious honey, only the super is opened and individual frames, heavy with honey and cone, are removed.

Much like their ant cousins, there are workers and drones. The drones are male bees that have no sting and gather no honey. They tend to the queen and all the larvae, build cones within the hive, and occasionally can be seen controlling the temperature of the hive by fanning air in or out. The workers on the other hand have both characteristics of collecting honey and stinging. There are many more workers than there are drones. There is only one queen.

A new queen can be created by the drones at any time by feeding one of the larva some royal honey. If a new queen is produced, she will fly from the hive and mate with a worker high in the air. They will swarm on a branch until a new hive is located. Usually, bees swarm in the spring at the onset of the honey flow. A queen will produce a couple of thousand eggs a day for about three years from her single mating flight. The nectar-gathering workers will live only about six weeks. During the nectar flow, as many as 70,000 bees live in a hive. The hive will shrink to less than 10,000 in the winter while living off their honey stores. Consequently, a farmer should never rob the hive of all the honey when it is close to winter; otherwise, the hive will starve and perish.

Now, in the great design of mother nature, honey generally flows most of the time, that is as long as there is vegetation flowering. The beautiful aspect of the life cycle is that most of mother nature has a sequence in flowering. So, you might be able to gather honey from clover, then move onto the black locust trees, then to the mimosa, then sourwood trees. The farmer needs the bees to pollinate the apple blossoms, his corn and wheat, and all the blooming plants in his vegetable garden. Without the bees there would be no fruit and grain crops to harvest since most plants cannot pollinate themselves.

The honey produced from the locust tree is opaque and black as molasses, while the honey from sourwood trees is transparent with only a slight amber coloring. The honey from cheery trees has a wonderful bouquet. As you would expect, some honey is prized more than others. The best is table-grade, while the bulk will be graded as commercial. The beautiful trick is to stack additional supers on the hive as the workers collect the honey all year long, so the honey doesn't have to be collected frequently. The honey is naturally separated as the flow moves from one form of flowering vegetation to another.

The bees will collect the honey from the nearest flowering plant. They have no favorites. Their behavior makes good sense when you think in human terms. Would a farmer collect firewood from a great distance when the same wood is available close by? There is a difference between hardwood and softwood. A pine tree is full of sap and burns brightly with a lot of smoke. The smoke carries creosote into the chimney, eventually depositing a residue layer of tar. If the tar gets sufficiently hot, it could ignite and cause a chimney fire. Hardwood does not contain as much resinous sap and soot. Therefore, it doesn't give off a great deal of light because it burns more slowly and has much less tar and smoke. In comparison, a hickory log would outlast ten pine logs of about the same proportion in a fire pit. For a long, consistent cooking temperature, the dense hickory wood is preferred for the pit-roasting of pigs and beef over a bed of coals.

Bees like to collect nectar from plants that have a long,

abundant flow. Some plants have a single flower which will stay in bloom until fertilized. This may be several days. Other plants have multiple blooms which last months as they sequentially unfold. The bees will communicate the exact location of the vegetation to the other bees by shaking off some of the pollen as they dance. The other workers gather about and read the direction signals, sample the pollen held in leg sacks, and instinctively know exactly where to go for the new source of nectar. Since their eyes can distinguish colors, the dancing bee might even be able to pass the precise flower color along to the curious audience bees.

Humans aren't much different. If some prospector came into a bar and started to dance a jig, after being primed with spirits, and would brag of the location where he had discovered a rich vein of gold nuggets, the bar room would be empty in a flash as every male would load his pack mule, grab his prospecting shovel, and head in that direction to stake his own claim.

Most of the bees around are of the Italian variety brought over by early English settlers. A swarm might be gathered and placed in a new hollowed log. Unlike most humans, two hives, one beside the other, can live in peaceful harmony even though they compete in the same territory. Taken a step further, two bees from different hives can be simultaneously collecting nectar, side by side, from an identical flower and not squabble. They are the epitome of compatibility. They don't wage ferocious war on one another. However, after collecting nectar, they always return to their own hive, even if it happens to be one that swarmed out of the other. They don't live long enough to carry grudges around.

If you go to messing with their hive, they get all over you unless you smoke them first. They worry more about the fire behind the smoke than they do about your messing with their honey. Some say the bees know if you're afraid of them. Some people walk right up to a hive, lift the top off the super and never get stung. There are photographs of people covered with bees from head to foot. They claim not to have been stung. But some contrary people can walk within fifty feet of a hive and have them light in their hair.

Now, when a bear gets the scent of bee honey, he is relentless. He will tear into a hive like his life depended on it. In defense, every worker bee will try to sting him. Even with bees all over him, the bear will keep digging for more honey. The bear is so well-insulated with a thick coat of hair that the bees cannot penetrate to his skin. Some bees get lucky with popping a stinger on an ear, on the nose, or on his tongue. He's got to be powerfully hungry because, you know, he's got to feel those stings. There will be dead bees all around him, because, when a worker stings, that's it. He has only one sting in him, then he's dead.

Allston Henslowe didn't know anything about bee habits when he went to steal the hive from Bartholomew. He didn't know about the smoking or that they nested inactively at night or that they were dormant during the frosty months. He didn't care if they had two, four, or six legs or wings. He wasn't concerned that bees have to make thousands of trips from flower to hive for a single drop of precious honey. Like the bear, he just knew he wanted that honey, and he wanted it in the worst kind of way. He may have been as determined as the bear, but not as hardy to withstand the ruthless defense of a brazen daylight attack. They swarmed all over him, causing the slow-footed, portly reverend to take off through the pasture with them in hot pursuit. He swatted at them and rolled on the ground like he was on fire. He pulled his coat over his head to hide his face. They got inside his shirt and up his pant legs. He danced like someone put a hot coal in his boot. When they had finished with him, he was covered with welts. He picked the stingers out one at a time, all the while figuring on a better way to get at the honey. He laid low for a few days while he rubbed himself with liniments of castor oil, wintergreen, and mustard paste until he could no longer stand the stench of the stuff. He had a tingling itch all over his body.

"Bart, how is the farm doing?" Cyrus asked.

"Well sir, got all the fencing up and have forty head of good beef now. I've got most of the pasture in clover, except one tiny spot that was my mother's flower garden. I kept my bees there until the other night."

"What do you mean? Did you move them?"

"Well sir, somebody done come along and knocked the super off the hive."

"They surely must have been hungry for some honey. Are you sure one of the steers didn't get loose and knock into it?"

"I'm purty sure it weren't no steer. None were aloose. And besides they ain't got a hankering for honey. I figure it to be a somebody because there was fresh tire tracks in the drive."

"I don't care for the tending of bees myself because I swell up if I get stung."

"Even when you put 'bacca spittle on the sting?" Bart asked.

"Yeah. I swell up like a cherry pit is under my skin."

"I was figuring on gettin' into the honey business when they swarmed. You know how them folk takes to the clover honey. They say it's the best there is to put on a stack of cakes."

"You're sure right about that, Bart. There is money to be made in beekeeping. And the bees do all the work."

"Well, they do most of it anyways. I got myself shut of them old holler'd tree trunks my dad set 'em in and got me some of dem new boxes at Palmer's place so'd I kin keep dem pupas out of the honeycomb. I figure, if'n I keep on splitting dem bees couple times a year and jar up and sell the honey, I might be able to fix up the cabin real nice if'n Eugenia - you ever have that talk with her about me a'courtin' her?"

The only thing that bothered Cyrus about Bartholomew was his lack of education. Bart was a simple dirt farmer and would always have his roots in the worn-out soil. Of course, that didn't mean that Eugenia couldn't educate him on reading and writing. There was no doubt he had the mentality for learning. And he was a good worker. He never got sick or lame.

But he didn't care about dressing up and going socializing at church.

"You know what I said about your attending church with Eugenia?"

"Yes, sir. I do recall your saying I needed to be more Christian. But can't a man believe in God and stay at home?" Bart answered.

"I know you have more logs in the fire than you can poke. There's no doubt that you drive yourself hard with all you do at the mill and your farm place. Sometimes I worry you bite off more than you can chew."

"Those beef need tendin', and when I get them bees all set up, they'll be like money in the bank. It don't take all that much to keep the place from growing up wild."

"But it does take you from Sunday churching."

"Yeah, I guess I could do better than I'm a doing at that."

"It's so important to Eugenia that, if you are courting, you sit with her at church. That way everybody knows you are courting her, and they expect you to marry. Right now, nobody knows you are courting but you and me."

"You didn't tell her my intentions?"

"Oh, yes indeed I did. But without you at church sitting by her side, in her mind, you haven't started to court. Women are like that."

"I guess you're right. I sure appreciate you telling me about women and how they think. They are a confounded mystery. I don't have no 'sperience with 'em," Bart summed up with a big sigh.

"So, we can expect to have you at church this Sunday and for dinner following?"

"Yes, sir. If that is what I'm a'need'n to be a'doin'. But, you mind if'n I come to the mill afternoon of Monday?" Bart asked.

"Tell you what. Why don't you take the Monday off after Church on Sunday? I think Eugenia will understand that you're giving up one thing for another. Don't worry about the mill work or your wages. We'll make things work out."

"God bless you, Mr. Boyd. Yep, I got to get used to saying that, God blesses everybody. And those who don't like hearing that, well, they can just be damned."

"I wouldn't use that damning too much. People who don't know they are not blessed certainly don't want to know they are damned. You're telling them so might cause some trouble."

"You mean like a punch-in-the-face kind of trouble?" Bart asked.

"Damned right," Cyrus answered.

The day after the next was Sunday, and Bart showed up at church as he promised.

Eugenia saw him riding up on Daisy. She waved and pulled up the front of her skirt so that she could run to meet him without tripping on the hem. Bart dismounted and tied the pitiful old mule to the hitching post just as Eugenia came to within touching distance.

"I had just about given up on seeing you here."

"Well, here I be. This old mule, Daisy, has one speed: slow. She has never been and will never be in a hurry to go nowhere. I got on my new shoes that don't squeak. And look a' here at my hanky. I forgot the Bible." He kicked the ground with his shoe. "I knew if I went back for it, I wouldn't be gettin' here till after folks were leaving."

She took Bart by the arm. "Don't you worry about the Bible; you can share mine. I'm so happy you are here."

She looked up at Bart with her light-blue eyes; they sparkled with excitement. She smiled the happiest smile Bart had ever seen on her face.

"Gee gosh, you look a-mighty purty all gussied up nice like."

"This is my new Sunday-go-to-meeting dress. How do you like it?" she asked.

"I've never seen such a pretty outfit on a woman. You look like a basket of flowers, and you smell real good too."

"Oh, Bart. You're teasing me. I bet you say that to all the girls."

"I ain't neither. What girls you talkin' 'bout? There ain't nobody in my eye but you. You're the one. I know'd that the first time I laid my eyes on you. I said to myself, now there is a real handsome girl if I ever saw one."

Eugenia could see the adoration in his face. "I'll bet Daisy is jealous."

"Shucks, Daisy ain't even a person. She's got no mind to her but hankering after feed. She won't hardly do nuthing 'less you yell at her. Acts like she's deaf in one ear and can't hear much from the other'n. Never you mind about Daisy."

"I've been saving you a spot with us on the pew for ages, ever since we pounded Reverend Henslowe. You know he's back."

"That's what I hear tell. Said he coughed up the money he stole."

"He was in a hurry to leave town because he had received word in the middle of the night that his mother had taken a turn for the worse. God rest her soul."

"Should've brung a jar of honey fer'em," Bart innocently said.

"No. We only pound the preacher once a year on the Sunday before Christmas."

A couple of women gave Bartholomew a slight curtsy as he and Eugenia came to the door. Their husbands gave him a hardy handshake and welcoming words.

As they walked down the row of benches, Eugenia leaned toward Bart, "Can you come for Sunday supper after churching? We'd be honored if you would break bread with us. Pa might even let you call the blessing."

"I know more 'bout eating bread than I does 'bout calling blessings. Maybe you best let him have a hand at doing it until I get the hang of what he's calling. I might call up the wrong thing right off the bat and everybody would think me the fool."

"But you will come?" Eugenia reiterated.

"You can count on me. I'll follow you right home like I was a lost puppy. Them biscuits your momma rolls out is 'bout the best in the nation, bar none. I ain't sampled all the biscuits there is, but I 'magine there ain't none better."

"I'd hoped you would come for reasons other than biscuits?"

"Oh, pardon me. I was meanin' other than sittin' with de finest folk there is in these here parts. Them biscuits comes next to the good company. I swear that's the truth and all the truth, so help me God."

Eugenia squeezed Bart's hand. His face flushed from her warm gentle grasp. Momentarily, his arm became rigid as though his joints had solidified from apoplexy of the limb. Slowly, he relaxed into the confidence of her comfort. He became less uneasy with his surroundings. Eugenia was digging into his layers as though peeling an onion, searching for the heart. Bart was beginning to discover a closeness which had been missing from his life. At first, he wanted to bolt and run. Gradually, he wished the feeling to never end. He willingly sloughed the hardened crust of apprehension. They sat side by side on the pew as though they were on an isolated island. The uneasiness of others watching evaporated into a blurry mist. The noisy clamor of voices and movements became a melody of love. Bart returned an intimate little squeeze and was passed back another. She smiled. He smiled.

Their eyes met casually. Bart timidly looked down at their intertwined hands. He admired the petite beauty of her delicate fingers. They were so unlike his own. Her nails were well shaped and even. He eased his head back to her's. Their eyes latched. Bart blinked more than usual. He could feel the blush rise in his cheeks and his heart take a leap. He saw her depth of calmness. He could see the purity of her soul. He stared with unquenchable wonder he couldn't release. She was like a vast expanse of shimmering water into which he had fallen. There were no limits to her boundaries. He was swept away, suspended, floating in a pool of love melt.

Eugenia was amazed much like a person seeing the vastness of an ocean for the first time. She was totally lost in his ubiquitous blue eyes as though she were glimpsing eternity. She felt as though she could step into them and be immersed in his soul. She saw his kindness and love. There, she saw his human life sparkle. Over there, she could see the touch of God at Bart's creation. There was the blessing of their children. Everything she had ever dreamed was in sight; she could almost touch them. The reality of time and place had lost meaning.

Suddenly, Ed Watson started a hymn on his accordion, accompanied by Aunt Carlotta, singing solo by his side. The fluid between them was interrupted. The brief moment was eternal.

Cyrus leaned over to Eugenia and asked, "I wonder where the Reverend Henslowe is?"

Eugenia hadn't noticed that the Reverend was nowhere around. She twisted her head in all directions looking. She asked Terry Goddard, who owned the lumber company and sat behind her pew, "Have you seen Reverend Henslowe this morning?"

Terry looked around just like Eugenia and asked Seth Palmer, who asked Cedric Oliver. Before you know, everyone was twisting and turning in their pew looking about for Henslowe. Folks were getting mighty itchy. Ed and Aunt Carlotta finished. It was past time to get the preaching started.

There were some words here and there concerning the whereabouts of the church fund.

Some joked of Henslowe's mother dying again. The congregation in general was restless. Cedric and Seth conferred on the subject of Henslowe's unexpected absence. They decided to attempt to carry on the service with some degree of dignity and decorum. Cedric called out into the congregation for the recital of Bible verses and hymn suggestions. Seth rendered an abbreviated and impromptu prayer for world peace. There were a few announcements concerning ailing members of the church. Finally, an offering was taken and blessed.

CHAPTER SIX

The Reverend Allston Henslowe figured the best time to get his honey was when everybody was someplace else. He knew where they ought to be Sunday morning. He also figured, once he threw the tarp over the hive, the roads would be clear for him to make a clean getaway. The congregation at Solid Rock Primitive Baptist Church would just have to get along without him because he had a more noble purpose than espousing Bible verses and telling the people what they already knew.

After he arrived at the Rombert place, he put a transparent silk scarf around his face and gloves on his hands. He was covered about as best as he could. There was no skin exposed. He studied the four hives and was perplexed as to which to take. He decided on the left center. He threw a tarp on the hive, wrapped it around and tied the bundle with baling twine. Some bees buzzed around the hive, but that didn't matter. He put the hive, heavy with honey, on the back seat of the Ford. Some bees followed the hive. Those inside were buzzing mad. Obviously, they didn't like what he had done.

Allston was raised in the city, so what he didn't know about country, especially bees, could fill a book. Bees are conditioned to attack black, that is their least favorite color. Black does not look like a fine nectar-laden flower. It resembles a black bear. Black bears are the bee's enemy. They destroy a hive. Bees cannot distinguish black from red other than the ultraviolet light they reflect. The red poppy flower is about the only one they visit. The remainder of the red flowers are exclusively visited and pollinated by hummingbirds. The color of red is one of those anomalies of nature, played between insect and animal. Most humans associate red with poison or blood. Red is a suspicious color, and like the devil, most be avoided. Not until several centuries ago were red apples and tomatoes determined to be safe for consumption. Bees associate black with death. Consequently, they will vigorously defend themselves in the presence of this color. White, being neutral, has the opposite effect.

Allston's habitual attire was the customary black coat and pants of a preacher man. Coincidental to bee predisposition? Perhaps. But nonetheless, quite unfortunate for Reverend Henslowe to be wearing black while trying to steal a beehive. They buzzed all about him while he spun the crank. They lit on him when he positioned himself in the driver's seat and engaged the motor car into the first gear. They gathered on the inside of the windshield. He shifted into second, then the high gear, and bounced on the road at the breakneck speed of twenty-two miles an hour. The more his vehicle bounced, the more the bees were jostled - just like a bear does when trying to pry open a hive. The more they jostled, the madder they got. Allston could hear their getting louder and louder the farther he dove.

He drove down the steep decline to Sabbath Creek and crossed the shallow bottom. As he drove up the opposite incline toward the ridge top, the gravity-feed gas line could not supply fuel to the engine. The Ford engine sputtered to a stop for lack of gasoline. He had to back down the incline with a dead engine, re-crank the motor while standing ankle deep in the creek bottom, turn the Ford around and back up the incline, thus giving the gas tank a higher elevation than the engine. During the process of maneuvering, the hive was jolted from the back seat and knocked forward against the back of the driver's seat, and the tarp opened in one little tiny corner. That one pinhole was all the ornery insects needed to find daylight.

The more bees that escaped, the more erratic Allston's driving became until he was weaving from one side of the ridge road to the other being distracted by the annoying bees.

The deep wagon ruts yanked him back into the groove. The bees didn't like being yanked either. Their buzzing increased in magnitude as more of the pesky little insects escaped from under the tarp. He kept the throttle wide open, thinking the more distance he could get between himself and the disgruntled people sitting on the church pews twiddling their fingers at Solid Rock Primitive Baptist Church, the better.

When Allston reached the top of the ridge some distance from the creek bottom, he decided to stop the car to push the hive back onto the rear seat. He thought he had the bees tightly secured inside the tarp. He erroneously thought more bees were joining the hive from all parts of the woods. He erroneously surmised they were being attracted by the buzzing distress call of those bound in the box. The fight for the honey became one man against the ill-tempered 70,000 insects. They were hot with a desire for vengeance. They were hitting his black coat and pants by the thousands. The weight of them on the sheer silk scarf was pulling it from his head. There were so many at his face, he couldn't see anything more than a thick blanket of angry bees.

Allston decided to put some distance between himself and the bees, at least until they calmed down, by running down the ridge line and back to the Sabbath Creek shoals and submerging himself in the protective waters. All the way to the shallow backwater creek, Allston was screaming profanities that the good Lord would not have appreciated. If he had stood still, the bees would have lost interest in him. A moving object draws attention, especially a black one. Alston also didn't know that bees aren't afraid of water or that they don't easily die from being submerged like a human. He couldn't completely cover himself in the shallow water, so the bees lit on an island of his clothing. He thrashed about trying to wallow out a depression in the creek bottom. He did manage to get his head under, which caused the blanket of bees attached to the thin silk scarf to adhere to his face. He snatched it off and shook the cloth vigorously, hoping to free it of the bees. His shaking attracted more bees to the soaked glove on his hand and to his arm. Every time he came up for a breath of air they were waiting, happy to have a target onto which to unleash their fury. For the first time in his life, Allston began to sincerely pray. He prayed for his life to a God who he had scorned and used for his own worldly gain.

Within minutes of Henslowe's hasty retreat, Cedric Oliver discovered him thrashing in the creek. He had only shortly left the abbreviated Sunday service. Most of the bees had returned to the canvas-covered hive on the back seat of Allston's Ford at the summit of the ridge. The Olivers did not know what sense could be made of the picture filling their eyes. Cedric tooted his horn. The Reverend rose from the water clasping his hat to his head with both gloved hands and the silk bandana spread across his face. He looked like a highwayman intent on ambush.

"Oh my God. This has been the most horrible day of my life," the reverend began.

"Reverend Henslowe, is that you?" Cedric asked.

"Of course it is. This has been one of the most horrible days of my life."

All the Oliver children climbed over one another to get a view from the side of the Studebaker. They stared, jaws agape and wide-eyed.

Cedric continued, "I... uh, we rather expected you at church earlier. Is there something wrong?"

"As I said, this is terribly disagreeable, most unpleasant."

"Sir, can you explain why you were in the creek just now? We heard nothing about your having a Baptism this day." Rowena Oliver asked.

"Don't be confused by what you think you see. I shall explain. While on my way to church this morning, I discovered, to my great distress, that a box of bees had been placed in the back of my motor car." With greater despair, he added, "I have been running from them ever since. I thought I could escape their wrath by submerging myself in these waters." Henslowe sighed, "They seen to have surrendered at the moment. My motor car is on the top of the ridge with the bee box if you care to inspect the veracity of my statement."

"Oh, dear sir, no. That's quite all right," answered Rowena Oliver from the Studebaker. "We shall take your word for the truth as you have spoken it. No further proof is required."

"They are no less agitated than I," Henslowe said as he brushed the clinging wet leaves from his coat. "I'm afraid this jacket is ruined, and my hat must be re-blocked."

"Could we do the service of delivering you to Butler? You might find someone there who is expert on handling bees," offered Cedric Oliver in a gentlemanly manner.

"That would be most kind of you," the reverend responded.

Rowena quickly said, "Do you mind wrapping yourself in this blanket? I mean to say, you, um, are a bit untidy at the moment." She handed her plaid wool lap blanket to Henslowe.

"Thank you. I am most grateful for the kindness of your favor," replied Reverend Henslowe.

"Do you have any idea how the hive might have found a home in your Ford?" Rowena Oliver asked.

"No, Ma'am. I swear I do not. The bees were all about me before I knew what was happening."

"And why, pray tell, are you on the other side of the shoals when this route is not connected between the boarding house and the church?" she continued her interrogation.

"When those bees started on me I just got all turned around. That's why I ran to the water."

"Closer water would have been the mill pond," she rebutted with the skill of a prosecuting attorney.

"I can honestly say, when bees are buzzing at your head, you don't know right from left, up from down. I thought if I got them into the woods, they would fly away into a home in the trees. That's the gospel truth."

Cedric interrupted her line of questioning. "In any event, I'm sure someone will want to take the credit for this deed. It might take a week or two; but, sooner or later, a tongue will wag, and we shall know the whole story, Reverend Henslowe. Mark my words," Cedric Oliver concluded.

"That mystery hive, my dear Mr. Henslowe, had to have had an origin. It could not have appeared from out of thin air. In a few days, we shall have the answer to this puzzlement," Rowena Oliver added.

"Well, I'm sorry you missed services. What were you going to preach on?" Cedric again intervened.

"I can tell you what I'm going to preach on next Sunday," Allston Henslowe spoke with considerable robustness.

Mrs. Oliver quickly commented, "I'll bet so. That should be tempered preaching."

"Well, here we are at the boarding house. I expect Seth Palmer can help you with the bees in the morning. I bid you fare-thee-well," Cedric lifted his hat.

"Thank you ever so much for your assistance. You have been most kind." With that, Henslowe retired to his rented room. He sent his clothes down to the landlord to be laundered and pressed. He ordered a food tray. His scheme had been foiled again.

"Good morning, Mr. Palmer."

"Good morning, Reverend Henslowe. Did you hear the President died?"

"What President?"

"Warren Harding, President of the United States."

"Oh, no. I didn't," Henslowe replied with a surprised look painted on his round face.

"Says so here in the paper. Calvin Coolidge is going to finish out his term. You'd know all about it if you hadn't missed Sunday meeting."

"That's why I'm visiting with you today. I need your advice and counsel on a matter concerning the removal of a bee hive that was placed in the back of my Ford motor car."

"I didn't do it."

"Mr. Palmer, I did not mean to imply you were the re-

sponsible party. I only desire your counsel on the removal of
the bees."

"You say, it's a hive of bees?"

"That's correct. I believe it to be a box full of bees wrapped
in a canvas tarp covering."

"What in the world is it doing in the back of your Ford?"
Seth asked.

"Eventually, I am sure the culprit of this prank will be
discovered, and the hooligan's motive will be known. But until
then, I am not able to approach my Ford. I cannot drive to
church. I no longer have the use of the buggy and horse. And
it's far too distant to walk."

"Well, I'll be. Bees, you say?"

"Yes. Quite right," he returned to Seth. "I would appreciate your advice on the name of an expert in the removal of the
bees. This is the purpose of my visit with you this morning, if
you please." Henslowe's face twitched with nearly every word
he spoke. The arrogant confidence Seth had seen in him while
at his pulpit had evaporated. A different man was addressing
him - one clearly in a foreign element.

"Well, I'll be doggone. I expect the bravest soul around
these parts is Benny, but he's up at the jail house on charges
of robbing Norma, the mail carrier. Now, the biggest fellow
around is Harvey Halloway, but he's off to sea going around
the Horn or helping to dig the Panama trench or something.
Hey Ed? You know of anybody around that has a fondness for
messing with bees?"

"Sure. Let me study on it a spell. Seems someone came
in here not long ago and bought one of them bee boxes. He's
a young'un - fresh and all - sat with the Boyd's girl at Sunday
churching. What's his name? I can see his clean-shaved face
and all. Don't reckon I knows where he's a livin' neither."

"Oh, you're talking about the lad at the mill. He's the last
of his kin here. They all died off and left him the place. His father and I used to trade."

"Do you know where I can find him?"

"I think I might. He lives by himself and is employed at the Boyd grist mill. You know where that is, don't you?"

"Yes, indeed I do. Would it be asking too much for somebody to give me a ride over that way?"

"We don't have any deliveries this morning as yet. You can set around for a spell or you might try at the feed store or down at lumber yard and see if anybody is going in that direction that you can hitch a ride with."

"While I'm here, can you tell me about bees?" the reverend asked.

"I never kept any. How about you, Ed? You ever keep any bees?"

Ed walked to the front door and spittled a long stream of dark tobacco juice from his cheek. "If I'd known you'uns gonna carry on such talking and all, I wouldn't of loaded a new plug. No sir. Came across some in a stump once. Seen some swarm in a tree branch. But I never fooled with them none," answered Ed Watson. Fearing Henslowe might wish to entice him into removing the beehive, "And I don't plan to neither."

"Okay. Thank you all the same." Allston Henslowe walked toward the feed store and repeated his story. He received the same response. At the lumber yard, Terry Goddard had a truck going out but not in that direction. He sent him down to the mill with a driver anyway after hearing he had already been at every store up town.

Everybody in town doing business or just plain loafing was talking about the hive in the Reverend's Ford. The new president wasn't much news. Whatever his name is, the new one, was a no-count Republican from up north just like the old one. There wasn't a confessing Republican in the county that anybody knew of except maybe the Cedric fellow, and he wouldn't say.

"Good morning, Reverend Henslowe. What brings you down this way in a freight truck?" asked Cyrus.

For the fifth time, Allston repeated his contrived story. It had become so familiar he believed it himself.

"Let me call Bart for you."

Allston realized quickly that Bart may be the same person as Bartholomew Rombert, his thief victim. Mr. Rombert's bees were in the back of his Ford. Allston spun around, searching. He had no means of easy escape. He decided to change his story. Cyrus Boyd returned with Bart. Eugenia was with him.

"Young man, it has come to my attention that you placed a hive of bees in the rear seat of my Ford. I am here to hear your confession."

"What?" Bart asked dumfounded.

"Those pesky bees assaulted all about my person and caused the abandonment of my personal property on the ridge beyond the shoals at Sabbath Creek bottom. I became negligent in fulfilling my obligation in the pulpit causing additional distress of the members of the congregation." Henslowe was flailing his arms as though he were delivering a sermon on piety to the devil himself.

"I don't know what you're talking about!" Bart exclaimed.

Eugenia and Cyrus were looking at Bart's perplexed expression. Knowing the Reverend Henslowe would not accuse Bart of such a prank without having proof, they were astonished that Bart would do such a thing to a man of respect and dignity.

"I think you do. I can understand your youthful age and a natural tendency for thoughtless foolishness. That can be overlooked and forgiven. But, young man, the repercussion of your action has caused those kind and faithful people at Solid Rock Primitive Baptist Church to forgo their Sunday preaching. My clothing is ruined. Least of all, I should mention the inconvenience of having to tramp around on foot without a means of transportation. What do you have to say for yourself?" Henslowe demanded.

"Bart!" Eugenia said in utter shock. "How could you?"

"I didn't do what you're a'saying," Bart defended himself.

"There is no need in denying what you have done, young man. Your lack of remorse is blatantly obvious. Lying is the devil's workshop. One ill-conceived lie will lead to the proliferation of a hundred more. Before you know, you will be leading a life of perpetual sin - sin without grace; sin without redemption; sin without morality in the face of God's will." Henslowe was sputtering hot pellets of saliva as he spoke. His face was red and distorted. The veins swelled in his neck and forehead. His arms continued to whip about in mock pugilistic battle.

"I think you have the wrong person, Reverend. I don't know nuthin' about bees in your Ford, and that is the gospel truth, so help me God. I swear." Bart turned to Eugenia, "You've got to believe me, I ain't had nuthin' to do with bees in his car. Honest."

"Uh, Reverend. What proof do you have to support your accusation?" Cyrus asked.

In exasperation from his ineffective oratory, Allston Henslowe suggested "If you can take departure from your employment, we can go to the location of my Ford, and Mr. Rombert can identify the hive," Henslowe said with certainty. He then muttered a low insult, "If he wishes to continue his protest of innocence."

"Where did you say the Ford was?" Cyrus asked.

"On the ridge above Sabbath Creek bottom."

"It won't take but a short time to drive there in the truck and get the hive out," Bart volunteered sheepishly.

Cyrus asked, "Bart, did you notice a beehive missing this morning?"

"No sir. It was dark when I came home last evening and dark when I left this morning," Bart responded.

"Well, let's run on over there before we get the mill up and going and see about this," Cyrus suggested. "Eugenia, you better stay around here to watch over things. Besides it would be mighty cramped with all four of us in the truck cab. Let's get moving."

Cyrus drove to the back bumper of the Ford. Bart jumped out behind Henslowe.

"Can't tell nuthin' with them all wrapped up," Bart said.

"But it sure looks like a hive full of bees just like you said, Reverend. How'd you figure them mine?" he asked.

"Mr. Palmer and Watson said you kept bees in a box about the same size as this one. I saw one in the store," Henslowe answered.

"They could be anybody's bees. All the boxes are the same size," Cyrus added in Bart's defense.

"I won't know for sure 'til I get back to the cabin and see if'n I got a bee box a'missing," Bart responded.

"I would appreciate the immediate removal of YOUR bees from this Ford," Henslowe demanded with poignant emphasis stressed on the intended ownership.

"Well, yes sir. I'll be glad to put 'em in the back of this truck and take 'em to the house. You can follow along and see for yourself. But I can say, Mr. Reverend, I didn't put this hive in your Ford, if'n they are mine or not."

Bart spoke forthrightly. He had never been in such an awkward, confrontational position with a fellow human. He was trying to handle himself with aplomb while maintaining respect for the reverend. He felt to offend the reverend was an offense against God. The thought never occurred to him that the situation might be a simple misinterpretation of facts. He would willingly take whatever punishment was prescribed by the reverend. Having Cyrus watching his every move and listening to his every word made him more nervous than Henslowe's tyranny.

Bart gathered a handful of pine straw and lit it with a red-tipped match he scratched on his coverall button. After the straw was burning really well, he snuffed it out and waved the smoke around the hive. He repeated the smoking of the hive several more times. "I'll retie this tarp around the box, so none of them can get out, then I'll put it on the truck. I'll have to smoke them again when we get to my place. 'Cus they'll be real upset from the bumpy ride."

"You do what you have to do. Then, we'll see whose bees these are," Henslowe remarked from a good distance. He hammered an invisible nail in Bart's back with the tip of his finger.

When they arrived at Bart's place, a hive was as obviously absent as a missing front tooth. Henslowe gloated. His accusation stood. His chest swelled, and his bottom lip pushed up in a display of arrogance. "See. I told you so. There's no doubt where this hive of bees came from." He strutted like a rooster and crowed like one too.

"I'm mighty happy to have my bees back, Mr. Reverend. But I will tell you again like I did before, I didn't put this hive in your Ford car. You're mistaken about that part of it. And that's all there is to tell. Exceptin', somebody would have to be awful mean to steal another's property and put it in another's car. It's done me a heap of harm as well."

"And you don't have any knowledge further than what you witness to?" asked Cyrus.

"No sir. There ain't nuthin' more to tell. Exceptin' I apologize to the reverend for whatever harm came to him and others from my bees. I'll be glad to pay it off and say the same to the church people right up front if that will make things right in his'n mind."

"There is going to be a lot of talk about this foolishness in town. Mark my words, they won't stop until somebody owns up to this deed. I'm a forgiving man. Your apology and denial of involvement are sufficient to put my mind to rest. I do think some mention needs to be made from the pulpit. As far as restitution for the damages to my person and belongings, I will be happy to square things with you for the harvest of your honey from this hive."

"Yes, sir. I meant to give you some more at the churching past, same as at the pounding."

Cyrus said, "That sounds fair enough to me." All the men shook hands.

When Cyrus returned to the mill, he explained the situation to Eugenia.

"You mean the only proof he had was that the bees belonged to Bart. That's all?"

"Yeah, that's about it."

"Bart had no explanation for how they got in the reverend's car. He was with us at church all morning when Reverend Henslowe says he discovered the bees in his car. Then Bart was with us until late evening and was here the first thing in the morning. He didn't notice his bees were gone, and he denies having anything to do with the prank. He apologized, and everything seemed to be forgiven."

"Who apologized?"

"Bart did. After all, they were his bees. He promised to give the Reverend Henslowe the honey from the hive as restitution for whatever damages had been done to him. That's where the two of them are now. Bart won't be in for the rest of the day or until he empties his hive of honey. I'd given him the day off anyway to tend to his beef since he… anyhow, he'll be here when he gets here."

"That was nice of him to offer."

"He didn't offer. Henslowe requested it."

"That's about as peculiar as the bees being in the back seat of his car."

"None of it makes any sense to me," Eugenia said.

"I'm sure sooner or later we'll find out the real truth."

Eugenia said, "For the time being, I believe Bart."

"I don't know what to believe. I figure if Bart had nothing to do with the hive, who did?"

"This is a small town and, like you said, it won't be long 'til we know for certain."

"In the meantime, let's get the rest of the wiring strung overhead and get the bulb receptacles in place. I want to see some lights on in here by the end of the week when them boys start at the second shift."

"We've got some milling orders to fill too," Eugenia said. "I can't run this place on my own while the two of you gallivant around the countryside. Oh, how did his place look to you?"

"Neat as a pin. He did a first-class job on his fencing, and the clover looks lush in the pasture," Cyrus answered. "And another thing. You got help here. You just got to ask them to do what you want, same as me."

That sneaky, conniving, con artist of a holy man worked all sides of the situation back to his benefit. He got his dozen mason jars of honey, but not the entire beehive. Before the next Sunday churching, he took off again for parts unknown.

CHAPTER SEVEN

Cedric Oliver announced at church he would "like to see a real pipe organ installed in the Solid Rock Primitive Baptist Church. The First Baptist Church up near the county courthouse has one, and our little church is just as good as theirs." He estimated the cost to be $3,500. He said he "will match dollar for dollar all money raised for the organ," which meant that he would be paying for half the cost. "To start the fund-raising off," he said, "there is going to be a turkey shoot fund-raiser at my place the last Saturday of this month. The prize will be a new Remington twelve-gauge double-barreled shotgun. The prize is worth nearly $30. All we need are 60 men paying 50 cents each to break even."

After church Bart asked Cyrus, "How do you win? They don't really shoot at tar-keys, do they?"

"You bring your own shotgun. They give you a shell to fire at a paper target. The highest pellet count wins. If there is a tie, then they step you back ten more feet. Some fellow from down past Davisville is supposed to be the best shot around. He's got a special gun all choked down so the pellets don't spread much at 70 feet. Seth has one for sale at his store that I've been looking at for some time now. About all it's good for is shooting skeet."

"What's a skeet, some kind of varmint?" Bart asked.

"Same as a clay pigeon."

"'Pigeons' I've heard of, but not one called 'Clay.'"

"I'm sorry. I thought you knew."

"I only knows what you tells me."

"They sling a clay disk about the size of a tea saucer in the air, and you shoot at it."

"Oh, like shoot'n' at a half dollar tossed up."

"About the same. Um, you ever hit a half dollar?"

"Never had one till I started here. I'd be darn if I would shoot at something I never had none of. I may look a fool, but that thar's a wasting good money," Bart replied.

"The target is about the same size"

"How fer off did ya say?"

"I think about 70 feet."

"That's a piece of cake."

"Speaking of cake, the women take cakes, pies, and cookies to sell along with handicrafts. They have a Bar-B-Que and sell dinner plates. We never had a turkey shoot to raise church money. Some say it's too much like gambling."

"T'ain't neither. That's a contest of skill."

"Could be, but for a sportsman unlike myself, it's a waste of hard-earned money."

"The church'll benefit. And a tar-key shoot sounds like a mess of fun. Reckon dat dere feller from down in Davisville will loan me his gun. I'd like to take a crack at one of them paper tar-keys."

"Won't hurt to ask. Shame to get beat with your own borrowed gun. I'd really like to see that. Don't count on it though."

"Why not?"

"One man is supposed to lend his shotgun to another that doesn't have one - kind of the unwritten rule of the sport. None of them want to get bested by another man. Just be sure and let him know you never fired a shotgun before. That should ease his mind."

"I 'preciate you're a tellin' me all the particulars. It sounds real inner-rest'n. I could use me a new gun. The slick-bore I'z got is a leftover from the war of that northern aggression on us. It makes a big sound but don't shoot straight. I only use it to scare bears away from my hive. Sometimes, I'll kick some dirt up under a fox that's trying to get in the chicken coop."

"If you can find that man and he does let you use his shotgun, I'll pay your fee just so I can have a good laugh. You ever shoot a shotgun?"

"No's, not I remembers of. But I figure they're all about the same. Ain't they? What's thar's to know?" Bart asked.

"When we go, you ask a few of the sportsmen that same question, and you'll get yourself a different answer from every one of them. That would be kind of like asking the Sunday Bible class how many times Jesus lifted his oars when he rowed across the Jordan River. Why, you'd get a different answer from every blessed soul of them."

"Who is this Cedric feller anyways?" Bart asked.

"He came here from up north somewhere - Pittsburgh or Ohio, I think. He got rich off industry. I don't know, never did ask. I never heard him tell exactly what got him well off. Maybe he got rich off selling supplies to the war. I heard of lots of people getting rich by staying home and selling supplies to the war department - good question. I'm going to ask him at the turkey shoot about his retiring here in North Carolina. You ever hear of the Vanderbiltmores?"

"No. Can't say I have."

"Those high-falooting folks built a castle over in the western part of the state in the mountain country near Asheville. Pictures have been in the newspaper out of Raleigh. It is supposed to be the biggest house under one roof in the state, maybe even the country. They made their money off of railroad trade and hauling passengers. He had a rail line laid right up to his house. Now ain't that something?"

"I've never been near one of them contraptions. Have you?"

"Matter of fact. I have. Back when I served in the army, they moved us from place to place in a train passenger car. We did about thirty to forty miles an hour, depending on how the land laid. We'd go down a decline faster than up an incline. If you stuck your head out a window, the wind would tug at your hair until you thought it might snatch the hair off your head. I never opened my mouth because I heard another soldier got blown up like a pig's bladder and nearly burst. It may have killed him."

Bart was getting bug-eyed listening to Cyrus carry on. He never heard such talk. He never imagined a human being going that fast. He didn't trust machinery anyway. "Thar's no way you could make me ride on one of dem thar trains of his'n. No sir."

"How about on an airplane?" Cyrus asked.

"Oh, Lord no." Bart abruptly jumped backward and turned pillow-cover white. "If'n God wanted man to fly, he would have given him wings and feathers to start with. No sir. Not a train and especially no ar'plane. A man's got's ta be touched in the head to get in one of them contraptions and fly higher than the birds. I'm going up one time; that's when I get called to Heaven on Judgement Day. Until then, my feet are going to stay right here on this ground for as long as the good Lord will allow."

"I've been thinking. We need to get ourselves another worker here to do your job so I can begin to teach you the grist business. You've been unloading, weighing, bagging, running the conveyor to the storage, loading wagons, and doing just about everything but work at the stones. If we could find the right person to do your job, I'd move you to Eugenia's job."

"What will she be a doing?"

"Way I figure it, the two of you are going to be serious at courting before long, and her mind just won't be on her work."

"We could put up a 'HELP WANTED' sign."

"I suppose so. But there would be too many interruptions and questions to answer."

"What do you mean?"

"Everybody that walks through here will ask how much does the job pay, for one. And I would rather not tell every-body what we can afford to pay. Besides I want to see what a man is worth before I set a wage. Some work smarter than others. Some look like they're working, but they're just moving about in circles watching the clock hands spin the day away. Your wage is higher than I've ever paid anyone else that worked here. One thing we don't talk about is how much money we are making. We just don't do that, otherwise people will think we are rich and we aren't."

Cyrus continued, "We just bought a truck, and now we are pulling electric lights. People are asking a lot of questions already. They are saying that if we can afford all those things, we must be overcharging them on the milling. They will begin to check with other mills for a cheaper price, and we won't have corn or wheat to mill. Before you know it, we will be out of business. Did you ever hear of the story about the horseshoe nail that got lost?"

"No. Not that I recall."

"After the nail got lost, the shoe fell off. After the shoe fell off, the horse went lame. After the horse went lame, the cavalryman had to fight on foot. Since he was on foot, he was killed. When he was killed, the battle was lost. When the battle was lost, the kingdom fell, and all because of one little horseshoe nail. Talking about wages is just like that shoe nail. Next thing you know, we are out of business. Now, you wouldn't want that to happen, would you?"

"Oh, no sir. Not at all. You can count on me not to say a thing about how rich you are."

"There you go again with that rich talk. That's exactly what I mean when I told you the story. Tell everybody how poor we are and how much we need their business. You've got a lot to learn about business. It's like when you go to buy a cow. You find everything wrong with the cow so the farmer will lower his price. He, on the other hand, will tell you how much butterfat the cow produces; how many gallons of milk she gives; how many heifers she's born and what great bloodlines she's descended from. Then the two of you dicker on the price, weighing all the good against all the bad until you come to a fair price. You never pay the asked price right off without bargaining. It's not proper. Some people will feel like you are cheating them without the haggling over price. They expect you to show some knowledge on the subject which will give or take from the price. You don't want people to go about saying how ignorant you are or how they bested you of a trade, now would you?"

"No sir. I never really thought about business being like a nail and haggling."

"That's what I mean when I say you have a lot to learn about the milling business. So, as soon as I can find someone that is willing to work hard for next to nothing in pay, I'll teach you about milling."

"How about convict labor? I heard they got some at the sawmill. They beat 'em and starve 'em and treat 'em like dumb animals."

"I don't want slave labor hereabout the place. To begin with, they probably aren't white, or they wouldn't be in jail. There's never been a Negro man in this county since it was settled by my ancestors, way back before the Revolution. I'm not going to be the first man that starts using the black people. What would people say of the Boyds? Besides, criminals have broken some law. I don't want any man that isn't a God-fearing, law-abiding person around my Eugenia. And I'll tell you another thing. This equipment is too valuable to place in the hands of a man that doesn't give a rat's ass if it works or not. One accidental wrong turn of the floodgate wheel and you got burnt flour. One little accidental bump of the thrust and locking lever and the stones will bite. When they bite, they can send off sparks that would ignite the flour dust, and the mill would burn down to nothing but a pile of ashes. I want the kind of man that you can put your faith in and who won't never let you down, for no reason. With these new electric lights, we'll be milling 24 hours a day, six days a week when the crops come in. We won't have to turn people away or hold their grain for weeks before we can get to it. No sir, we'll mill like there was no such thing as day and night."

"Mr. Boyd, we'll be needing more than just one spare hand to get all that work done. When will a man eat or sleep?"

"We'll go in shifts. It only takes three people to run this

mill. With a spare person, we'll have three on and one off. When the one off gets his rest, he'll jump in and relieve another to rest, and so forth until there isn't a grain left in the bins or a wagon standing at the door."

"What if'n one of us comes down with the pox or the influenza and has to stay in bed for a week?"

"I won't allow it."

"Mr. Boyd, I think we need three more people, not just one. The reason I say that is because we'll need you the most rested of them all so you can go about giving orders from one place to another and meeting the farmers and haggling the price. Next is, I'm not wantin' Eugenia and, I suspect, you neither, to be a workin' as hard as you are a sayin'. She is a girl and a might pretty one at that. I don't want her all roughed-out like an old field hand. With no rest, she's likely to get irritable and ornery like a mule. I admit, we got the wagon load before the oxen on these here 'lectric lights and all."

"We have camp meeting in a couple of weeks. The mill will be closed down, and we can go shopping among the idle for maybe two helpers while we're there."

"I hear the Dotson boys are out looking to hire on somewhere. They were by here week before last with a wagon load of corn needin' crackin'. Ole man Dotson got so many young'uns off them three wives, he's going to make them boys pay him for his'n place."

"He'll just drink it up in shine."

"In no time, he'll be beggin' them boys to take him in. That sure would be a twist of a turn 'bout."

"Serve him right. You get what you give in life. They say the fruit doesn't fall far from the tree. Well, I'm here to tell you that nut tree bloomed some strange flowers. I'll put the word out to Seth that I want to talk to them about employment. We're clear about having just the right kind of worker here, aren't we?"

"Oh, yes sir. There ain't gonna be no grit in your meal 'cause I'll be keepin' my nose right to your grindin' stone so's there ain't no sparkin.' And them that does get on here better bring a cot, bathin' towel, and kiss their mommy goodbye."

First Baptist Church dispatched Reverend Elijah Thomas in the afternoon of the third Sunday of the month in the absence of Allston Henslowe for the purpose of consecrating certain sacraments and tending to ecumenical duties. There were marriages, infant Baptisms, and the acceptance of new members which needed proper officiating. He saw over the burials in the church cemetery when needed.

The actual preaching was left up to the rotation of the church board of elders. It always gave great amusement to the congregation to see one of their own, pink with embarrassment, fumble through the service order. The reluctance and incompetence of the elders to stand before the congregation on a given Sunday and preach the word of the Lord from the Bible, often extracting an incidental confession of a personal trespass, greatly increased the fervor of the board in securing a permanent arrangement with a man of the cloth. In the meantime, wives and children would squirm in the pews in fear or in response to any reference to domestic behavior. Many tongue-lashings and stoic silences were delivered to fathers on the trip home in an attempt to balance the tabulations of personal tribulations less to his credit and more to theirs.

Supper would invariably be late, sparse, or not served at all. The children, plucky with the persimmon bite of adolescence, would often cry, scream, throw tantrums, drop dishes, and somehow manage to extract a modicum of revenge for any household reference made during their father's discourse at the pulpit.

The domestic civility of a wife or children was usually the topic of an elder's assigned Sunday. There were no female elders. This topic of choice was presented entirely from the father or husband's point of view of a home being a man's kingdom. A wife was totally subordinated to her husband's authority in all matters. Women had only recently been given the right to cast a ballot for a political candidate of their choice. The female gender had always been considered a second-class citizen. This predisposition had not changed at Solid Rock. There was tumultuous domestic turmoil following the pulpit lectures.

For instance, Seth, who was relegated a single chair in his household and dominated into pale submission by Sarah and her two obedient daughters, was the epitome of a henpecked husband. When he rose to the pulpit and expounded from 1st Peter, Chapter 3, Verse 7, concerning a woman being a weaker vessel, his chair was removed from the house and placed in the mule's stall inside the barn.

All other activities were set aside the following week because the camp meeting was underway doing the Lord's work. The rustic open arbor was surrounded by rows of shabby log and clapboard cabins in which families temporarily resided. Preachers and choirs came from all over the state, rendering their best performances from sunrise until well into the evening. Allston Henslowe's absence was not missed. The elders of Solid Rock Primitive Baptist Church were busy interviewing prospects to fill the pulpit. Cyrus and Bart talked to young men who might be willing to do mill work. The youngsters were running about everywhere playing tag, hide and seek, seesawing on boards, playing war with sticks, swinging on ropes tied to tree limbs, and scampering from one cabin to the next. Old women sat on their porch rockers pretending to be sewing or shelling beans and peas, but mostly viewing the constant parade of people passing their perch. Something always caught their critical eye which necessitated a comment.

"Oh, would you looky at that'un. Her skirt is way too short. You can see ever bit of her ankles. Why she ain't nuth'un but a floozie gallivantin' 'round here half dressed."

"Oh, my gracious goodness! That'un got way too much bosom showing. They look like ripe melons 'bout to explode our from her blouse. She needs a shawl to kiver herself with. I just can't look no more. She's downright indecent from over-exposure."

"Them's the ugliest pair of shoes I ever did see. Who

would want red leather? They just ain't practical for nuttin' but show."

"Looky how that one has her hair all done up on top of her head. She's trying to be taller than that man. Before long a pigeon's going to be nesting in that tangled mess. Does it look like she's got dye put in that hair?"

"Euw-we, looky at that'un. She done plucked her brows and painted new ones up in the middle of her forehead like one of them Hollywood movie stars."

"That young'n could shore use himself a haircut. Why, he looks more girl than boy. A good mother wouldn't let her young'uns go a roamin' around with folks not knowing."

"Look at them geezers over yonder tossin' them horseshoes. They got bellies on them bigger than my sow. If I were a bettin' woman, I'd say they hadn't hit a lick with a stick in years. Dem 'spenders is the onlyest thing holdin' dem pants from falling to their feets. Tossin' dem pony shoes is 'bout all dem good fer. I'd give 'em ,nuther five minutes and they'll be snoring from overwork."

Eugenia prided herself on parading Bartholomew before the rows of cabins. The public latching of arms was the equivalent of an engagement announcement. "Eugenia, bring yo' young man over here and make an introduction," one of the old ladies called.

Eugenia would do as they had requested to satisfy their curiosity and quiet their speculation.

"Sugar-pie, yo' lookin' so purty with yo' hair all combed back so I'z can see yo' face. Yo' gots such a nice ribbon in yo' hair. You'z gets purtier by the day."

Another matronly woman in a calico dress with a skein of yarn in her lap said, "You remind me so of mother Martha. How is she taking lately? We never see her abouts. We do pray her health be restored."

A third nosy brown hen with her fingers busy snapping pole beans chirped in, "Now, tell me about your beau and the particulars. I declare you'uns just make the sweetest lookin' couple in all the campground. You thinking about tying the knot? He shore is a fine-looking man, so tall and big in the shoulders and all."

After Eugenia and Bart completed their respectful visit as proper etiquette required, they continued to mosey along the path fronting the cabins arm-in-arm. The women continued in their pecking - for a while the subject was Eugenia and Bart, but they moved onto their own children's courting behavior and finally to their own. Each one had a different story to relate or rendered comments on another's tale of freshly dusted memories. Each seemed to compete with the other concerning whose beau courted the hardest. They began talking about which gave the best gifts and had the most prosperous farm. Their prattle was not lost, without nary a pause, when an occasional grandchild wanted a snack or a soft, warm lap on which to nestle or dry a tear.

They could hear the preaching and singing just fine from where they sat. They found no need to move closer or under the arbor. They had been to more camp meetings than they wished to count, doing so would give a true indication of their age - which was nobody's concern. They settled the count clearly as to who had the most children living and dead. They counted up their grandchildren and great-grandchildren. They settled on who had the most blood relatives at the meeting. Each claimed a notoriety in some insignificant way even if it came to who had the most male or female offspring. They all claimed some relations to a famous officer in the Revolutionary or Civil War, the latter being more worthy of credit.

In the week of meeting, the women exchanged every recipe in their inventory of culinary arts. Verbally they buttered and salted popcorn, made every flavor of ice cream, baked every kind of pie, and pulled taffy into peppermint sticks without ever having actually done so. Between imaginary delights, they would snuff their lower gums and purge themselves into spittle cans. Some lit corncob pipes with their husbands after the supper meal.

Some feller came around to make photographs of families. Getting the children to sit still and the endless primping and pruning consumed most of the sessions in front of the camera than the snap of the lens' shutter. Others waited in line, as did Eugenia and Bart, to have their turn. The barber had just freshly shaved Bart's face and plastered his hair with balm to slick it back. Eugenia put on her best dress and a fashionable bonnet borrowed from one of the Wilson sisters.

As the week wore on, more sawdust had to be hauled from the mill and spread on the paths leading to the arbor and along the cabin paths. New straw had to be laid on the cabin floors. Daily sprinkles of Red Devil lye were applied to the privies to abate the flies and odor. Cats with fat bellies laid in the sun, giving the little field mice full advantage to pillage through the cabins. Occasionally, you could hear someone yelling at a mouse. The resulting clamor of attempting to extricate the creature from a hiding place didn't seem to arouse the interest of the cats. They were pretty much worthless after the first day or so.

Bart and Eugenia finally had an opportunity to stroll away from the watchful eyes of the elderly who, by general rule, maintained the decorum of youthful interests in matters of the flesh. Their courting had advanced from the stage of an engaging look into each other's eyes, to having spoken a casual word or two about mill interests, to the touching of warm hands and the latching of arms. Eugenia was anticipating the intimacy of an embrace, perhaps a kiss. The one along the road, while Bart captured the swarmed bees, didn't count as a proper kiss in Eugenia's way of thinking. Neither had been lost nor given themselves to another in the way of romance. Being a novice in matters of the heart and body, Bart needed guidance and assurance from Eugenia. Both were nervous as they strolled the path into the woods.

"Bart, I've had the most wonderful time these past days being with you. You are such a gentleman."

Bart began to think that he should not push for the kiss

least he would not be a gentleman in her eyes ever again. "She might think me ill-mannered," he thought. He hoped, hour after hour, as they paraded around the grounds for a signal that Eugenia would invite him into an embrace. He began to think she might be more comfortable being more like a sister or a good friend that happened to be a boy. He knew he was not her confidante, only Mrs Boyd could fill that role. She did not share secrets with him that began or ended with, "Promise not to tell."

"Did you ever look at all the different kinds of bark there is on trees?" Bart casually said while trying to get his mind off the foolish idea of a kiss. "There is the smooth bark of the cherry tree. See there," he pointed forward in the distance. "The hickory has a bark like it's got muscle under its skin. The pine has flakes of thin-sliced, well-done beef flank. And that sycamore there has ridges of bark you can cut off and use for a fishing line bobber. The bark off the oak can be ground up and used for tanning leather skins. Someday, I want to get me a book that gives all their proper names."

"Maybe mother has one you can study."

"Let me do the asking now. Don't you go running home to fetch a book because this is the first time we've really spent time together, you know, alone. It seems strange not having the grind of the mill in the background. It's so peaceful here. This really is a nice change," he said.

"Do you miss the mill?" she asked.

"No. Not at all. It's nice to get away. I'd much rather be with you than a sack of meal any day," Bart diplomatically said.

"I guess I can take that as a compliment being compared with a sack of corn meal."

"I didn't mean… well, what I meant to say… uh, I don't know how to say what is in my heart."

"Let me try to say it for you."

"Can you see what's in my heart?"

"We'll see. Okay, here goes. I feel like there is nothing else in the world but you. I think about you all the time even when

I don't see you," Eugenia said.

"Yes! That's what I mean."

Eugenia continued, "When I get up in the morning, I dress for you. I brush my hair for you."

"Yes! And when I going to the mill, I'm not really going to the mill at all. I'm going to see you at the mill. And when I have to leave the mill, it's not the mill I'm leaving, it's you I say goodbye to, not the mill. I don't know why I said anything about a sack of meal. Just forget I said anything about a sack of meal. I don't know where that came from. It just popped into my stupid head."

"You've got a beautiful head. I adore your head. You're not stupid. You just aren't educated. I think stupid means more that a person can't learn new things and ways. You've taken to milling like you were born to it. A stupid person couldn't do that."

"You have such a beautiful way with words. You can explain things so clear. You can talk black clouds into sunshine."

"Now listen to yourself. You're the one that's almost poetic."

"You're the one with good grammar. All I needs to do is listen to you talk and you make me a gentleman when I'm just a country bumpkin. I want to be the best gentleman that ever held your arm."

"Oh Bart, we are so much alike we belong together like a matching cup and saucer." She took his hand and placed it around her waist. She leaned back against a large white oak tree pulling him with her. He braced himself against the trunk for fear his weight would crush her or spoil her dress. They were face to face. He could feel the warmth of her breath on his face.

"You smell good, like a field of flowers. My bees would be all over you if you got near."

"What would they do?" Eugenia asked.

Bart face flushed. He could feel the heat rise and burn his cheeks. He fell into her eyes. She was beckoning him forward.

Her lips were blood-red and inviting.

"Tell me. What would they do to me?" Bart watched her tongue slowly roll to moisten her lips.

Bart felt dizzy. His legs could hardly support him. Eugenia put a hand to the back of his head and pulled him closer. "Would they take their little mouths and kiss the flower?"

Bart could feel a surge of electricity excite every cell in his body. He was tingling all over as though the bees were pushing him forward to the sweet red petals of her mouth. Their lips briefly touched. This wasn't enough for either. They craved more honey. They were driven by the magnetism of nature. Bart wrapped his arm around her neck and pulled his flower to him. She surrendered and tightened her arm about his waist and head until his body fully pressed against hers. He kissed at her ear, her neck, her eyes, and back again to her eager moist lips. Neither ever felt so alive, so in need of each other. Their breathing became heavy and deep. They were running with wild pounding hearts.

Bart was the first to pull away. "I think we are about to sin. I've never lusted such." He was trembling as though soaking wet on a bitterly cold day.

"I think we better stop until we are, um… I mean, until… I'm so fuzzy-headed," Eugenia answered.

"Are you sure?"

"No. I want you in my arms forever. I want your baby more than anything I've ever wanted in my life."

"You are my baby. You are all I ever wanted. I want you more than anything else. Will you marry me? Will you be my wife?" Bart asked.

"Yes, with all my heart. This day and forever," she answered.

Bart fell back into her embrace more intensely than before. His body was pressing hers. His hips spontaneously began a rhythmic grind. His breathing became rapid. Suddenly, he moaned and collapsed onto the ground in a faint.

"Bart!" Eugenia exclaimed in a whisper. "Are you all

right? Bart! Talk to me."

All Bart could do was moan. He pushed himself up on his elbows.

"What happened?" Eugenia begged.

"Shh, you'll draw a crowd over this away. I think passion took me. I'm so weak that I can't get myself upright. Now I see why married folk," Bart had to stop for a gulp of air, "keep a bed together. I wish I had one under me," he took another gulp, "right now."

Eugenia was proud their passion had made Bart faint. She took it as a sign that he really loved her. "You won't need a bed. I'll be under you."

Bart rolled over on his stomach and covered his face. "Oh Lord, don't be puttin' dem thoughts in my head. It's gonna be all I think about now. Every time I look at you, I'll lust."

"I'll make you a good wife."

"If'n I ever get my strength back. My knees is just a wabblin' like I just wrestled a bear."

"What kind of thing is that to say to your fiancée? First you tell me I'm a sack of corn meal. Now, you're comparing me to a bear?" Eugenia lectured sternly.

"I mean to say that you got kisses stronger than a bear hug. They done made me wet my pants. Fiancée? What kind of word is that?"

"That means we are going to get married."

"I hope sooner than later," Bart responded. "I gotta gets me some fresh drawers. And I will tell you a 'nuther thing. We need to quit playing this bee business until we get that knot tied, or I won't have strength enough to work. I shore hope they found themselves a preacher for the church. We'z gonna be needin' him right off. Lordy woman! I've never been so torn up like'n this before in all of my life. What'd you done to me? I can barley push one foot in front of the other'n."

"I just collected me a little honey from your sweet little flower," Eugenia remarked coyly.

"Lordy, I never knew the bees were having so much fun.

If'n I could come back in life as a bug, I know for shore I'd pick a bee."

"Then, I would be your flower."

"Now I know what the birds and bees is all about. I always wondered on that," Bart jokingly quipped.

"My mother tells me there is more to it than kissing," Eugenia whispered to Bart as she laid her head on his shoulder.

"I'd be afraid to know what more there could be to sparking."

Eugenia thought for a second. "You've seen a bull mount the back side of a cow, haven't you?"

"Yeah. They play like that all the time."

"Well, that's where the calves come from."

Bart stopped walking and turned to Eugenia. "You mean to tell me they are making calves that away?"

"You didn't know?"

"No. I only knows what you're a tellin'. I thought they was a playin'. I never know'd dem playin' had a thing to do with calves."

"Nine months after they play, a calf is born."

"You're fooling me. Nine months? Ain't no wonder I never added the one and ones together to make three."

"Where did you think calves came from, the grass they were eating?"

"I never studied on it. I thought they had 'em when they needed to have 'em. I knew they needed to have a bull around, but never knew why. Oh, I think I'm beginning to know what having babies is all about."

"It has a lot to do with why your pants are wet."

"Eugenia!" Bart gasped for air. "You shouldn't talk such." He pulled his tucked shirt out from his pants to cover himself. "Everybody will know what we've done back at that oak. You best go on back separate like. I'm a gonna stay behind 'til the dark sets in. If'n anybody asks about me, you just tell dem I'm a collectin' firewood an'll be along directly. I couldn't bear 'em thinkin' I shamed on you. Go on, be gone."

Eugenia dusted her dress and pulled at the shoulder puffs as she reluctantly followed Bart's instructions. He was right, but she longed to be in his arms. "There would be time for more of that," she thought, "the next time I have him alone." Her heart swelled with the thought that she could now call Bart her fiancée. She couldn't wait to tell her mother and father that Bart had declared his love and proposed marriage. She thought about being called Mrs. Rombert. She thought about herself and Bart being called Mr. and Mrs. Bartholomew Rombert. Her head was busy with thoughts of having a wedding. She was floating in the dream of his passionate kisses. She could taste him on her lips. She could feel him on her. She wanted him so badly her mouth went dry.

"Where's your beau?" asked one of the ladies.

"He wondered off somewheres. I believe he meant to get a change of clothes," Eugenia answered.

"You keep a close eye on him so he don't stray off to another's arms. Ya hear?"

"Yes'um. We're engaged to be married. I don't think he'll be running nowheres except to the church. My Daddy is looking for a preacher now."

"You ain't in trouble. Is you, girl?"

"Oh, no Ma'am. I ain't never laid with a man. I've been keeping myself pure. Same thing with Bart. He's pure as Pa's flour."

"That's a good girl. The two of you will have a nice life."

"Yes Ma'am. Thank you, Ma'am."

CHAPTER EIGHT

"First thing you need to know about millin' is to get the grain in and the meal and flour outs of here quick as you'z able. You give them what they want, or, if'n they brings it, ask 'em to wait for us'n to grist it while they're a waitin'. They'll be all lined up like on the road anyways socializin' or sellin' hams, eggs, vegetables, quilts, and what-nots. They may go off down to the general store or get a haircut or go to banking or buying shoes, you know what I mean. You have to have their job done when they gets back so's they can get on home. You tell them about how long you think it's going to be before we finish their job. Understand that so far?"

"Now, if'n you wants to unload and trade for what's already been milled and put in bins, you weigh out their load and send it up to the granary barn. We got feed bagged out in hundred-weight and mixed six different ways depending on what they gonna be usin' it fer. There ain't nuthin' complicated 'bout that. They'll tell you just 'bout all you need to know."

"I think I've got it. The grain goes in here, and the bags of flour and meals come out there. Right?" Jason jokingly asked.

"Don't the two of you get smart with me. Ya hear? I'm old enough, and you'uns are just babies. I can turn you over my knee and give you a good whacking whenever I take a notion. And don't you talk no money neither. You leave that to Miss Boyd or Mister Cyrus. They do all the givin' and takin' of money."

"Now listen up, you little children. This ain't no Sunday school class. Pay attention to what I'm a sayin' 'cause I ain't gonna repeat myself over again on the same subject. Ya Hear? Now, ever so often you gotta clean the trash from that Frits wheel. If a big stick gets caught up and the wheel stops a'turnin', everything comes to a stop. Now, looky here. When you're climbing about at the base of the dam, take that shotgun. It's full of rat shot. That pool down below is full of copperheads. They's after the mice. Watch where you'uns puts a foot 'cause them rocks is mighty slippery. We shut the water gate from the inside crank next to the grist. Don't neither one of you touch that wheel. Ya hear? 'Cause when we do that, your job is to get that bucket of grease and mop dem bull gears, dem ring gears, and the bevel gears down below, and any place where two pieces of metal is a'touchin' one nuther. The transfer box takes special oil. I'll show you that later. Don't go puttin' grease where lubricatin' oil goes or vicey versey."

"Now most important, when we are at the milling, don't you light no match. This here place is full of flour dust, and all it takes is one little spark and the whole place will blow to kingdom come. Don't you go touchin' nuttin' 'less you told to. Can you keep all this in your peanut heads?"

Jason said, "I think so. If I have any questions, I'll ask you."

Jackson, the younger of the two at fourteen, shook his plump head. His belly-fat jiggled. He seemed to be more absorbed in cleaning dirt from under his nails with a jack knife than listening to Bart's profound oratory exposition.

"You and your brother can be a big help, or you can be a lot of trouble. And I ain't gonna stand for no foolishness. There's always somethin' that needs tendin' around here - belts break, screens need cleaning, or we need to bag out the bins. I don't want to see either one of you'uns sitting on your backside pockets."

"Mister Cyrus is teachin' me about workin' dem stones and the roller mills. So, I'm gonna be learnin' his job while you'uns are gonna be learnin' my job. With these lights here about, we'll be running this place around the clock when the crop wagons come rolling in. Don't you go play'n hooky on me, or I'll skin your hides and hang 'em right here to dry and for the flies to walk all over."

The boys looked at the mill siding not knowing if Bart was serious about their skins.

As Bart turned away from the boys, he heard a thunderous crashing sound. The building shook violently. Something was wrong, bad wrong.

"Good God Almighty!" He rushed to the grist where Cyrus had been working. Eugenia came a second later. The boys stayed where Bart had them sitting, knowing if they were needed they would be called. Otherwise, they would be in the way.

The French burr roller stone, which Cyrus had recently dressed with Milpecks to sharpen the furrow stitching, balanced and leveled on the four-arm rynd, had broken. A large chunk of the dense rock skirt had torn through the wooden apron and shot across the mill floor just as 17 rpms had been reached. Cyrus had been in the process of setting the tentering gap between the runner and base stones. The 19 by 42 inch, 6,000-pound roller stone would have to be replaced. The task ahead of them was difficult simply because of the stone's weight. The water gate was shut. Everything came to a quiet standstill.

Eugenia said, "Dad, you could have been killed."

"A piece of it caught me, but I don't think it hurt," Cyrus said.

Eugenia and Bart looked at a torn section of Cyrus' pant leg. They could see his torn flesh and a trickle of blood.

"Dad! You're hurt."

"It's nothing," Cyrus said bravely. "I've had worse."

"Let me see it," Eugenia demanded.

"It's just a flesh wound. Nothing's broken except that stone. Pay no mind to me. I've got more pants at the house. Let's get the tongs and start lifting the roller off," Cyrus commanded.

"Dad, we could replace it with the blue granite."

"Then, we wouldn't mill the wheat."

"We should have enough in the bins to fill grocery orders

until we can get another burr runner up from Charleston - that would be better than a week though," Eugenia said hesitantly.

"I could buy three of those Rowan County granites for the cost of this French burr. But they make the best flour," Cyrus added.

"Why does a burr stone make better flour than a granite," Bart asked.

Eugenia said, "Don't ask."

"No, I would really like to know. I need to know this."

"Bart, get them two young boys to haul that chunk of stone to the spillway," Cyrus ordered.

When Bart returned, he persisted in asking about the burr stone.

"There are several reasons," Cyrus began. "First, the French burr stones have a better consistency. The granite may have soft spots that give off grit into the flour."

"Oh, that's not good," Bart observed.

"No, not at all, Cyrus continued. "Nobody likes grit in their biscuits. Secondly, the burr will hold a better balance and is therefore less likely to bite the base stone. Biting can cause grit and spark if it gets to wobbling."

"Not good either," Eugenia added.

"The most important difference between the two stones is the milling temperature and consequent fineness of the flour. If there is too much pressure or too high of an RPM, the flour will overheat by friction. The scorching will not only kill the flour and give it a bad taste, but it won't rise properly. A lower grinding temperature allows enzyme activity to continue, and that is important."

"What does that mean?" Bart asked.

"Makes the biscuit flaky and taste better," Eugenia answered.

"Oh. I never baked a biscuit."

"If you come to the house before sunrise Sunday, Aunt Carlotta can show you all about baking biscuits. She makes the lightest biscuits in the county. The ones I bake have to be buried in the back yard for a week before you can eat them," Eugenia exasperatingly moaned.

"Before dawn? I think I'll pass on that. You can bring me a basket full of them to church, and I'll be glad to eat them for her."

"All right, you two. Let's get down to work."

"What's the difference between regular and self-rising flour?" Bart asked.

Cyrus explained, "Every miller has his own secret formula. In a nutshell, all-purpose flour doesn't have soda in it."

"What's the soda, do?" Bart asked.

"We put Regent V-90 phosphate, salt, and soda in the self-rising flour, but leave out the soda in the all-purpose flour. When the soda, salt, and phosphate react, little air bubbles are trapped in the flour dough. That's what makes bread and cakes spongy and porous."

"In the old days, the women would mix them up to suit their own taste. They call the soda baking soda, but it's nothing but sodium bicarbonate. The baking powder has soda, phosphate, and salt in various combinations, depending on which store brand you buy, but they are all about the same," Eugenia added.

"They mix them at home for whatever purpose they are baking. For instance, pie crust has different characteristics from loaf bread. It's all flour any way you sift it," Cyrus said.

"Hmm, I like anything baked," Bart said.

"And that is what keeps us in business - making the best flour, meal, and feed that can be had from any mill in the county," Cyrus said, somewhat summarily and ending the conversation.

"And customer satisfaction," Eugenia added.

"I declare. The two of you have my mouth all slobbered up for some buttermilk biscuits and red-eye gravy. Um, wouldn't a plate of them be tasty just now with a cup of hot coffee?" Bart grinned from ear to ear.

"They always say, the way to a man's heart is through his

stomach," Cyrus said to Eugenia.

She quickly responded, "The two of you must think I've got nothing better to do than to stoke up an oven and pop out biscuits when you take a hankering. Here we are just about shut down, milling nothing but air, and the two of you are swapping recipes like two old housewives at the camp meeting. I ought to get those two young boys in here to run this mill with me. They would be a dang sight better than the two of you."

"Looks like she is about to retire the both of us. Come on, let's get out of here," Cyrus said.

At first Bart was hesitant and looked at Eugenia for an explanation.

"Go on, git. And don't neither one of you come back until you're fit to work."

Bart fell into Cyrus' footsteps, out of the mill, past the two boys.

"She wants you in there to change out the runner stone," Cyrus told Jason and Jackson. They jumped up and ran into the mill past Bart.

Cyrus paused to give Bart the chance to catch up. "That will teach her to keep a civil tongue in her mouth. Let's get that coffee you were talking about. That will give her time to cool down some before we go back in and tackle the real work. You got to take a firm hand with a woman, or else they will get accustomed to running all over you until you are nothing more than a squeaky mouse of a man, like that Seth Palmer. I know a thing or two about what I'm saying."

"I hope you're not gettin' me in trouble with her."

"Let her pitch her fit and take it out on those boys. We sure won't be around to hear it. It'll probably do them a lot of good to get scalded by her right quick up front before they get lazy habits. Besides, I don't like to work when I'm mad at a piece of machinery. I might try to punish it when it has no feelings and can't ouch back. Then, I might do more damage than good. Best to let it rest for a while and get my head clear about wanting to fix it."

"What do you think we should do first after we have our coffee?" Bart asked.

"I've got another apron in the top floor storage. You get it and bring it down. The old one is torn to smithereens. Let's get out the broken burr and bring in the granite runner just like Eugenia said. That will please her because we will be doing what we would have done anyway without her telling her opinion on the matter. I'm going to let you set and balance the stone. You can set the tentering gap for corn meal and open the water gate. Then, you open the chute and begin gristing. The first couple of bags will have flour and corn so it will be a premium blend meal. After that, it will all be feeder before we reset the tentering for meal. How does that sound?"

"Fine. But don't you go wandering too far off. I'll need you a spell to talk me through all these changes. I don't want Eugenia breathing hot flames down my neck. What about us gettin' those boys to move the stones in and out for us?"

"That will be okay. That's what we told them, but you better watch them closely. If one of those stones gets away from them and starts rolling on its own, we'd have to get a brace of mules to bring it back. On second thought, I'm just about willing to let it go for a while, this being Friday and all."

"What do you mean?" Bart asked.

"We can hang a sign out saying we are closed. I'm not sure if I want to go to all the trouble and strain to fix things right away."

"How come? You not feeling well?"

"No, it's not that. We got the turkey shoot and barn dance tomorrow, and the mill won't be running anyhow. Why slap wear ourselves out doing all we have to do and not being fit to take a swirl at the Virginia reel? The way I see it, it's an either-or situation."

Bart suggested, "I was thinkin' we might get as much done as we can, you know like the movin' of dem stones today while we got the boys, and leave all the piddlin' stuff for Monday. Besides, I doubt Miss Martha is much for dancin' anyways with her health being so poor and all."

"Don't let that fool you. She can find more reason to keep me busier than a bullfrog when the termites are up. I feel like a jack-in-the-box, jumping up for punch, jumping up for a napkin, jumping up for a crumb of cake, jumping up when someone comes to greet her. There is no end to it. I might get a dance with one of her sisters, Eugenia, or a niece. By the end of the night I could wring the sweat out of my shirt. No sense in having two hard days in a row."

"Why don't you go on to the house, take a rest, get yourself a bath and all dappered up fer tomorrow, and leave us to do what we can with dem stones. Then we'll call it a'quits."

"Don't let Eugenia push you further than you want to go. On second thought, why don't you send her on up to the house so she can start to get all dolled up for tomorrow. Remember, you still have to go back home, get yourself a good night's rest, and be at the shoot at sunrise."

"Moving that stone is still a'botherin' me."

"Me too. With that piece missing from the skirt and if the iron hoops busted loose at the rivet, it might not roll just right. If it tips over, all hell might break loose. That floor is braced with 24-inch pillars and cross-bracing, but you might still lay a trail of planks. What's left of the stone must weigh better than a ton."

"Shoot, is that all! I'll just toss it on my back and walk it out."

"Ha. You and ten others. What a day! You're a good kid. It will be a pleasure to have you as a son-in-law. Miss Martha and I always wanted a boy like you."

"How long must a guy live before folks stop calling me a boy?"

"Well, let me spell that out for you. You go from a boy to being an old man when you don't have any seniors. Those two kids at the mill, for instance, will always be kids or boys to you no matter how old they grow or how many children they father. There will always be the difference in ages between you and them. They think of you as a man and me as an old man. That's about the only difference. Now, a gentleman is altogether different from all that. They don't work like we do every day with our hands. Take Cedric Oliver for instance. I don't believe he worked a day in his life. I doubt he ever had a callous on his hand from chopping and splitting wood. He's the kind of man that you won't find in a trench with a carbine. He is back at headquarters figuring on who is going to live or die by shuffling a stack of papers. He's nowhere around when the mustard gas comes rolling in the trench and your buddies are coughing their lungs out and dropping like flies. I don't mean to say he's a bad man. He just a gentleman and gentlemen don't get their hands dirty."

"Where do they get their money from?" Bart asked.

"From book learning. They've been well-schooled at universities. They make money from what they know and sometimes who they know. You could stand to do more reading yourself, you know. Culture comes from knowing stuff that nobody else cares about. You get that out of books and traveling. I've always wanted to look at London and Jerusalem. I think it is too late for me to be a gentleman, like Mr. Oliver, but I sure would like to make some of the guys pause in their checker game when I tell them about towers built with marble that stretch up to the sky as far as an eye could see."

"Is there really such a thing? I can't imagine anything that tall. They must stake it with wires to keep the wind from toppling it in a storm."

"I wish I'd the money to send Eugenia over there for her schooling, but I needed her here in the mill to help me keep things running. I've never paid her a skinny nickel for her work. I've kept her fed and clothed and a roof over her head, but she doesn't have money. I mean, she can buy what she wants, but she has never traveled and seen the world. It's too late to make a lady out of her. She's just one of us everyday kind of people. She thinks about right now, where as Mr. Oliver thinks about next year and beyond. Take for instance, the church organ. He had it all figured out way in advance on how to raise the money."

"There's good in that. When you can create somethin' with your hands, I don't mean corn-husk dolls, but somethin' like a bag of Boyd White Flour that everybody needs, there's a certain amount of pride in doin' that. I'd rather be makin' flour than readin' books and dreamin' about marble towers."

"The day will come when you look back on your life's work and think that you could have done better for your children."

"I promise you, Mr. Boyd. I'll make you proud of me. When Eugenia and I get married and have children, you won't regret having me as a son-in-law. I'll make good on that promise."

"Have you ever been to a library?" Cyrus asked.

"Not that I know of."

"They have books you can borrow, read, and return at no charge. There is a world full of information just on grist-milling alone. People read all about a subject and invent better ways of doing something that no one else thought of. They invent a machine like the cotton gin, get a patent on it, and become a millionaire selling the idea to other people. Take that Sprout Waldron name off the roller mills from Hanover, Pennsylvania. How much do you think he gets on every machine he sells? I'll bet, if since we have four of his machines and there are 20 mills in the county and 50 counties in the state and 40 something states in the union, that adds up to a ton of money. I'll bet he's a millionaire. Do you see what I'm talking about?"

"Yeah. That adds up to a lot of money."

"But you have to be an engineer and a draftsman to figure everything out so that somebody can build the machine from your pictures. You get that kind of learning from a university. The thing about going to a university is that you aren't working, but you're spending money to learn how to make money. I guess a man could get a part-time job somewhere to help with expenses."

"Makes perfectly good sense to me. When Eugenia and I

have children, one of them will be an engineer. I thought they drove trains?"

"There are all kinds. That guy that invented refrigeration, now there's something. I've wanted that for a long time. I'll get me a great big one and open an abattoir."

"Never heard of one. Is it like one of them thar places where monks live?" Bart asked.

"You mean an abbey?"

"Yes, sir. I think so."

"No. Not at all. It's a slaughterhouse. We could process the animals, place them in cold storage, and butcher off the meat to suit folks' needs. Think of all the people around these parts that need fresh meat who don't have a beef in a pasture or hens in a coup. Think about the farmers that slaughter a hog and need some place to keep it in storage until they need it. Maybe they only want half and want to sell the other half. We could do that."

"I never put my mind to thinking much about it. I guess I do need learning and book reading," Bart remarked with a tinge of guilt at his ignorance.

"A mind is like a muscle, the more you work it, the stronger it becomes and the more work it can take on. After studying various subjects, you discover they all have similarities and common differences. Take farming of livestock for instance. Beef is about the same, but different from sheep and goats. What you have to do to get a good crop of corn is about the same but different from oats, wheat, and barley, right?"

"Yeah, I see what you mean, same but different."

"That's my whole point. Processing grain into flour and meal is about the same as processing animals. Granted there are different skills, tools, and equipment involved but, dang nab it, everything is about the same."

"I just never thought about it like that."

"But you agree, don't you?" asked Cyrus.

"Oh, yes. I think you are a genius on figuring. I was wondering which direction we wanted to take the milling business.

Do we want to buy another mill, process more grain, grow our own grain, ship to wholesalers in train loads, or what? I think we need a plan of where we want to take this business. I hear about mills closing all over the place. There are too many around, and people are buying flour from way off out-of-state because it is a penny cheaper on the pound."

Bart continued, "Some of them thar flour bag fellers say the business is consolidatin'. I think that was the word they use. There're big accounts and small accounts. We're a small account. That's why we don't see dem much. They're busy with the big accounts. Now, I asked myself, why are we a small account? Who are dem big accounts, and why are they big? They must have done somethin' we ain't a'doin' to get thataway."

"Part of the problem is the government taxing. We have to pay $1.50 for every bushel of wheat we process and sell and 75 cents on every bushel of corn. That's ten times more than we make. We're being taxed out of business. I can't accumulate enough money to make improvements. If I lie or don't keep good records, they'll put me in jail. That's why out-of-state flour is cheaper. They aren't being taxed to death like we are. That's why so many mills are quitting. You aren't being paid for your time after having to sell to meet their price. Times are just getting bad. I think those Republicans are making us pay off the war debt all by ourselves."

"That just ain't right, and you know it," Bart was getting angry. His face was all screwed up like he sucked on a green persimmon. He clenched his fists and was ready for a fight.

"Don't get all worked up. There isn't anybody that will take the responsibility for lying on the taxes. They do that in the Capitol building, a whole gang of them. Not a one will say to your face that they are for the taxes we pay. Yet, they sure know how to spend the money on big government buildings and roads to get to them."

"Wish they would build some of dem buildings around here. We could use some of dem new roads here abouts. The ones we got ain't no good for drivin' on in the winter time."

"Are you registered to vote?"

"Not that I knows of."

"All you need is to be a landowner to vote. Your property is in your name, isn't it? I mean you pay property taxes on it don't you?"

"Lord yes. That's all the reason I had to come and work for you so I could get up the tax money."

"Next election we'll vote for the guy that will repeal or lower the tax on our business."

"How will you know who that would be?"

"I'll get Seth Palmer to read the papers and ask about. He knows who is supposed to represent us at the capital."

"I best be gettin' back to the mill and get dem stones all changed out."

"Can you handle it?" Cyrus asked.

"Yeah, I think so. I should be able to figure out how to put one on by taking the other off."

CHAPTER NINE

The Reverend Henslowe headed into the north Georgia country and sought to be a pulpit relief preacher. He made the rounds to most all the small Baptist churches in Clayton, Cornelia, and Dahlonega collecting a few dollars for his preaching. When he rolled into Gainesville, he knew the town was large enough to exploit the excellent healing virtues of his magic elixir.

He had flyers printed and rented the American Legion building for a week where he would set up Henslowe's Holy Healing Crusade. He mixed a batch of the hard cider, wintergreen mint, and honey from one of Bart's mason jars. He sampled the concoction expecting to be flamed with exhilaration. He felt nothing. He took a larger swallow, still nothing. He mixed a batch from another mason jar and sampled it. The results were the same. He took samples from all the jars and made little batches. He was disappointed that none had the euphoric effect he anticipated.

The reverend was furious beyond consolation at having been duped by the young man in Butler. All the money he had spent on flyers and in renting the largest building in town would do him little good without the magic of the special honey. People wanted miracles and would have paid him their fortune for his cure. He would have to settle for nickels and dimes which wouldn't cover his costs.

Allston returned to the American Legion post and asked for his money back. They informed him of their policy to refund only half of his payment since they had turned down other conventions interested in the rental of their meeting hall. He said he would take it for only the first four days because urgent business had called upon him. He told them his mother had suddenly taken ill, and he must tend to her health. They agreed after his giving the gravest of news. Nothing was more important than a son tending to a mother in her final sunset hour of life.

Without his elixir Allston Henslowe went to the pulpit and began a three-hour oration on the great healing powers of the believing faithful. Vigilant prayer and constant reading of the Bible could and would restore one's health. During the final hour, he invited people forward and laid his hand on them in the name of the Lord that they may be healed. Some claimed to feel better, but not like the effect they would have had if given a dose of his elixir. For his night's work, he collected nearly five dollars. The donation was sufficient to cover the cost of the flyers, but not the hall rental.

On the second night, the crowd was larger. There were a few familiar faces waiting for his call. He furiously preached on the seven deadly sins. He fell upon his knees and passionately cried. People stood, shouted, and waved their arms above their heads like antenna wishing to attract a flash of lightening. He whooped them good that night and collected better than twelve dollars, half the cost of the hall.

On the final night, the hall was full of preachers from all the denominations within fifty miles. They wanted to see his hellfire first hand. He gave them their money's worth. He jumped, gyrated, and danced from one side of the platform then back to the other. He fell to his knees and cried. He buried them all in prayer and brought them back to life again with fervor resiliency. He whipped them like coach horses into a gallop with high-pitched screams, then slowed them to a trot. He groomed them with soft words of praise then fed them with rhythmic rhetoric in prayer.

His thoughts were on Bartholomew Rombert and the honey hive. His thoughts were on the fortune his elixir would bring to him. He reveled in the anticipated fame. He would try once more, vowing to get it right. All he needed was the right honey, not just any honey. He knew Bart was playing with him. He suspected Bart knew all the time as he eagerly gave him the honey from his hive to placate his injury and appease his soon-to-be father-in-law. Yes, it was a game to Bart, Allston thought, a game that he would lose. Nobody had ever outsmarted him, and nobody ever would.

Late one Saturday Cyrus, Martha, Aunt Carlotta, and Eugenia left to visit Martha's sisters. They would stay overnight, which meant accommodations for Bart would be inappropriate. Besides, if he went along, he would crowd the women. He took a notion to spend his free time and go bee hunting. He folded a comb of honey in a piece of waxed paper and stuffed it into his pocket. He rode Daisy to the other side of Butler away from all his own bees. He staked her on a long tether in an open field and walked to the creek bottom. He continued down the creek until he spotted a honeybee collecting water at the edge of a sandbar. He sprinkled a little flour on the bee's back and waited. He counted to 1,264 before the flour-dusted bee returned to the exact location for more water. He calculated in his head the distance in yards to the hive by taking the number and dividing it in half, since the bee made a round-trip. He figured the bee could fly three yards a second, so he tripled the number. He divided the figure by two because he could step off a yard in two strides. He guessed the hive was about 900 steps away from where he was squatted.

Bart placed the comb of honey on a bark slab on the sand bar by the stream. He sat close by waiting for a bee to light, gorge itself, circle three times as it gained height and take off in a bee line toward the hive. More came by the plenty. Bart got their directional bearings by spotting a tall white oak on the ridge line. He picked up his bee box and headed toward the oak.

He looked right and left along the bee line until he heard one buzz past him low to the ground. He saw a hollowed-out spot in a dead-but-standing gum tree. He set his box nearby and pushed the gum over carefully so as not to smash the combs too badly inside. He lit a pile of pine straw and dead leaves to create billows of smoke. He then hacked open the hive with his broad axe to expose the comb. He quickly lifted the queen from her brood and shook her off in front of the new box. He was stung a bunch of times. He placed her on the box platform at the brood. Both she and the attendant drone bees crawled in. He lifted the cover and tossed in some honey comb and a large chunk of their brood comb. When he returned two days later, all the bees had followed the queen into the new hive. The workers had quickly moved comb and honey. Bart plugged the entrance slot and carried the new hive to a stand next to his other two hives.

Two days later a swarm of bees lit in a branch of an elm tree by the mill road. Bart ran down to Palmer's to get another bee box just like his others.

"You must be starting an apiary down on your place," Seth deduced.

"I ain't got nuthing to do with apes. Whatcha talking about?" Bart was astonished Seth would think he had anything to do with monkeys, gorillas, or apes. "You sure I'm getting the right kind of cage? I've been using them for keeping my bees."

Seth couldn't hold back his laugh. He was making Bart seem a fool. Ed joined in the laughing even though he didn't know what Seth was talking about either. "No, I didn't mean anything about apes… ha-ha… or gorillas… ho-ho… or monkeys… he-he. What I meant is that a collection of beehives is called an apiary." Seth continued to laugh loudly. Ed's eyes widened in surprise. He was just as much a fool as Bart. He didn't say anything; he went to get the bee box, which is what he always called them, same as Bart. "Same as a collection of flowers being called a garden. A collection of beehives is an apiary."

"That's nice to know. If they called them a bee-iary, everybody would know what you're talking about. It don't make no matter whatever you want to call them. I've got a swarm hanging on a tree branch and nothing to put them in. Just gimme the box and have a blessed day."

When Bart returned, the bees were still in swarm. Eugenia was standing guard so no one else would try and claim them. He shinnied up the tree like a monkey after coconuts and straddled out the limb like a polecat. The bees were more interested in swarming than in protecting themselves, so they didn't take much notice of him. Bart raked them off the branch with his bare hand into a flour sack and came back down the tree. He opened the top of the box, lifted the screen, and dumped them inside. Others, which had still been flying around, landed on the entrance platform of the brood and crawled inside with the queen.

"I'm going to let them settle overnight here before I take 'em home."

Eugenia watched, awed by Bart's cunning bravery.

"Bees can tell if you're afeared of 'em. When they do, they'll pop you all over. Now don't go and try to pull out the stinger." Eugenia took a few steps backwards. Bart continued "Take your jack knife and scrape the stinger off. Some 'bacca juice will ease the sting a might. Some say bee stings are a remedy for arthritis and rheumatism, but I never had such ailments. Now, 'bout the honey. Clover is good, but some folk swear the sourwood, being clear and light, is the best. Some folks truck their hives up here around the mountains where the sourwood is thick and set their hives out. They do that about June 20, I hear tell. Depends on the moon. All you got to do is put a super on the hive, and the bees will fill 'er right up, and the honey won't be mixed with what is down below. Some farmers will pay you to bring bees to their crop for fertilization. Wild honey ain't no good but for house use 'cause it'll be black and won't have no-good taste. Some cook with it or use it to sweeten mash in making shine."

Bart continued, "There is a mess of superstition about robbing of the hives. Some say to rob after the first frost; some say on a full moon; then others say on the first day of April. If you do it late in the year, you got to leave enough honey in the hive comb for the bees to live off of, or else come spring they will all be dead. I should be able to get 40 to 50 pounds from each hive, maybe 200 pounds all together, depending on how many supers I add on. Seth said he would buy all I brought him for up to 25 cents a pound if it all was clean of comb and dead bees. Fifty dollars! That's good money."

"When we set up housekeeping, I want you to know all the monies Seth pays for the honey is yours free and clear less what I owe him for the boxes. It won't be much at first, but I plan to have a bunch more of the hives. They call a collection of bee hives an apiary. So says Seth. They ain't no trouble. You got to keep the moth larvae out. They'll eat up all the honey and fill the super with webs. But the bees do most all the work. All we have to do is collect the honey gifts and put it in jars for Seth. His money will help you buy little what-nots that you might need. He was telling me to put out some apple trees. What do you think? Do you like apples?"

"What kind?"

"I don't mean those hard horse apples. I mean nice plump green and red ones for eatin' and bakin' in pies. You pick them out, and I'll get them in the ground. There ain't but one apple tree on the place, and that's at the graveyard. Some pears and peaches would be nice. The snow and sleet came so bad the year before last that most of my apple limbs snapped off. They say apples won't grow on new wood. So, we've got to wait on the suckers to get stout enough to hold 'em."

"Did you ever do much canning?"

"Mother does some. She likes preserves of strawberries, figs, blackberries, and huckleberries the best. I help wash, clean, and blanch them while she boils the jars and lids."

"Am I boring you with all this talk about bees and apples?"

"No. Not at all. Well, maybe. Actually, it gets me all flush thinking about keeping house with you. I've never lived a night away from home before. Would we have the same room to sleep in?"

"I kinda thought we would have the same bed."

"Oh gracious. Now, I'm flushed all over. I think I better sit myself down for a spell before I faint out right."

"I'm sorry. Did I do this to you with my talk of sleeping in the same bed?"

"Oh, my head is all swimmy like."

"Here, let me hold your hand."

"Oh. Oh, my goodness. Please, don't. Stop. Oh, please don't stop. Oh, please…" Eugenia fell backwards onto the ground. "Take me in your arms."

"You're a shiverin'. Your hands is cold as ice. And your face is all flushed up. Have you taken sick? Eugenia, open your eyes."

"I'm on fire. Kiss me before I die. Kiss me now, quickly."

Bart leaned over her and gave her a tiny little peck. Eugenia gripped him around the head and pulled the kiss deep and hard to her lips. Her breath was hot on his face. She took several short breaths like they may be her last to expire from her chest. She held him tightly, her body spasmed and quivered as she felt his weight drop on her.

"Hey, you two!"

Eugenia's eyes popped open, and her grip loosened. She thrust Bart off in embarrassing fright.

"What're you doing over there?"

Eugenia sat up abruptly. Her pallor turned from crimson to white.

"I think she's a'dying," Bart answered. "She took a spell and fell right off in a faint. I was trying to revive her."

"Sure looked like something different to me. But then I have seen some strange things in my life, but never next to a beehive alongside a road."

"I'm feeling much better now. A sip of water would help clear my mind. Bart, can you help me back to the mill? I would certainly appreciate your assistance."

"Reverend Hinslowe, is that you?" Bart asked.

Eugenia said, "I believe it is."

"What you doing back in these parts?"

"I'm buying gasoline for my car. I traded off my buggy for a Model T Ford."

"Is it running all rightly? It ain't torn up or nuthing, is it?"

"No. I just returned from down in Gainesville, Georgia, where I held revival. I gave the folk there some of your fine honey, and they would sure appreciate your giving them more."

"My honey is promised to Seth at his grocery."

"I do want to talk to you about that first jar of honey you gave to me at the pounding. What was it that made it so special over the other honey you gave me in retribution of my injuries?"

"Just what kind of injuries did you exactly have, Reverend?" Eugenia asked. "I never got that clear in my mind. And nobody around these parts ever could explain how Bart's hive found its way into your car."

"Some things are always a mystery. Aren't they, Sugar? Like the two of you laying here face to face, one on top of the other right here on the ground," the reverend savagely retorted. You better dust yourself off. Your hair and backside are covered with leaves. Folks are going to be guessing at what you and Mr. Rombert was doing on this roadside."

Overlooking the reverend's comment, Bart answered. "That was some of the honey that came out of my dad's old beegum. It was full of poppy honey off from my mom's flowers. I still got that beegum stashed in the barn if'n you want to study on it."

"I sorely would like to get some more of that poppy honey. When rubbed on a sore it's got certain healings properties. Do you think my request would be possible for you to honor if I overlook what I saw going on here between the two of you?"

"You wouldn't!" exclaimed Eugenia.

"I'll have to think on it a spell. How long so you figure to be around these parts?"

"That, young man, is difficult to say. The Lord moves me in strange ways. Do you mind if I stop by your place Sunday afternoon, now that I know where you stay?"

"Well, Reverend sir, you would have a better chance of finding me tending to Miss Eugenia here than there."

"I really must be going back to the mill," Eugenia interrupted.

"Are you courting one another?"

"Nice seeing you, Reverend. Maybe we will see you later," Bart added.

"I certainly hope so."

As Bart and Eugenia walked to the mill some distance away from the hive, Bart began to explain, "I think there is something suspicious about that reverend wanting my honey."

"I just don't care for that man anyway which way you slice him. He's a stomach ache through and through. Did you hear the way he was trying to extort you by telling on us? Why is he interested in the dark poppy honey more than the clear clover? That seems stranger," Eugenia remarked.

"I can tell you one thing that's for sure. I had to fence off the poppy flowers from the steers 'cause when they ate those flowers, they would lay next to them for hours. Then they would get up and eat more until they plumb fell over again. There was something unhealthy about eating those flowers. I think they are poisoned."

"If they are, then wouldn't the honey be poisoned too?"

"I reckon. I had to keep them steers from nibbling on 'em. The flowers spread out a bit to the fence line, but a few of 'em don't seem to hurt 'em much. But if one gets out, he'll eat at 'em until he falls over in a sleep… act like they are drunk and all. Those steers aren't stupid. You got to watch 'em."

"Ask Dad or Seth about what's in a poppy to make the beef cattle go lazy," Eugenia suggested.

"They are just like the reverend, they won't leave 'em alone," Bart added.

When they returned to the mill, Eugenia immediately interrupted Cyrus, "Dad, Bart wants to ask you a question about poppy flowers." Cyrus was after Jason and Jackson for letting the stitching machine run out of cord.

"Listen to me, boys. You never, I mean never, walk away from a machine that is not ready to use by the next man. If it is broken, you fix it or get one of us to come over here. If it is out of adjustment, you make it right so the next person won't have to figure out what is already in your head. I'm disappointed in both of you for letting the line run out and not threading it back. You ought to be ashamed of yourselves. The only thing I can think of that is worse is using up all the paper in the privy and not telling anybody."

Turning to Bart, "What?"

"Maybe I can ask you later when you aren't hot and bothered," Bart sheepishly responded.

"Sometimes I think those boys don't have a lick of sense. They have their minds on everything but what they're doing at the moment. Turn them loose in this place for a week, and nothing would work. Everything would be torn up and broken down. And they never put a tool back when they use it. You got to hunt all over the place. It would take them a tenth of the time to walk a tool back to its home than to drop it where they last used it. Might as well sell this place for scrap wood and iron for all they care."

"We should have been here rather than gallivanting after the bees. You'll never guess who we saw," Eugenia said.

"Oh, let me guess. President McKinley and a tribe of shaved monkeys riding pink elephants," Cyrus answered with obvious irritation at having to play Eugenia's guessing game.

"I believe one of those bees must have gotten under your collar," she curtly responded. "The Reverend Allston Henslowe, that's who." She jiggled her dad's surprise.

"Well, I'll be. What's he doing around these parts again? I swear he's like a bad penny."

"He was asking Bart all about his honey. He wants more, some from the poppy flowers."

"Well, that little snake. So that's what he's up to, peddling honey."

"Not really. At least, I don't think so. He says the honey is a cure. What do you know about poppy flowers? Bart says his cattle nearly fall dead when they get into the poppies. He had to fence them off."

"Every plant has a unique sap. Some sap is dried, powdered, and made into a poultice for healing. You know like mustard. Some sap, like the maple, can be used as sugar sweetener. Some is downright poison like ivy and sumac."

"Poppy, Dad. Get to the point"

"I'm getting to that. Just hold your impatient little ponies."

"The sap of the poppy makes into an opiate."

"What's that?" Bart asked.

"It'll make you drunk as shine with no hangover."

"Well, no wonder the reverend wants that poppy honey," Eugenia said with a sassy surprise.

"And I'll tell you another thing or two," Cyrus continued. "After you get some, all you want is more and more. That's why it's against the law to buy or sell it without a doctor's approval at the apothecary. However, those soda bottlers put a taste of cocaine in their drinks. That stuff is just as bad. Like smoking the tobacco leaf, once you get started, it's hard to quit. That's why we call them bad habits. Of all people, the reverend should know all about bad. That's his trade, trying to make good out of bad, if you understand my meaning."

"You don't suppose he's using the honey himself, do you?" Bart asked.

"I don't know anything about him except he's in the soul-saving business."

"Well," Eugenia added, "I think he is up too no good. What was Bart's hive doing in the back of his car? And then, he turns around and wants all his honey. There is no good going on with him. I tell you. Mark my words when I say he is going to be more trouble."

Bart said, "Those poppy flowers are in bloom now, but 'em bees just mix the nectar in with the clover honey. There ain't no way to keep the bees on one or the other since I put in that clover field."

"That reverend will certainly be disappointed that he can't get any more of your pure poppy honey. I wouldn't be surprised if he doesn't go out to your place and take all the poppy pods after the petals drop. Most all the sap is concentrated in the pods."

"He is a no-good scoundrel if he tries," Bart said.

"You can't be here and there at the same time. And he is footloose and fancy-free to come and go when and where he likes," Eugenia said.

"When I get home this evening, I'm a'gonna harness up Daisy and plow my momma's posies right under the ground so that varmint can't poison people with the sap juice."

"Good idea. And if he comes to the house looking for you, I'll keep him busy till dark," Eugenia added.

"I tell you somethin' else. I'm goin' to move dem hives all around the perimeter of the pasture. You know, outside the fencin' so the steers can't tilt 'em over. I was ponderin' on it the other night. Dem bees ought to be spread out some so's they all ain't dipping into the same clover time and again lookin' fer somethin' 'nother bee already took. They always chase after the nearest flower, you know, whether it's got nectar or not. With dem all spread out, each hive will have their own territory to collect nectar. I oughta to be able to get twiced the honey collected from each little bee than I do now. With dem all spread out and tucked in the woods away from the house, the reverend won't know where I hid 'em.

"Do you think we should get Sheriff Hothgart after him?" Eugenia asked.

"He hasn't broken any law that I know of. He gave back the money he took from the church," Cyrus answered. "He's not a dangerous man. I mean, he doesn't have a violent nature. Let's just wait and see what happens."

"Maybe he's done wrong in another town or state and they are hunting him. Maybe there's a reward for his capture," Bart suggested.

"Well, if there is, it's got nothing to do with the milling business. All he seems to want is poppy honey and that's no crime. I'd leave it well enough alone. No sense in cluttering up our minds on what might be when we got these two rascals here that's driving us crazy right under our noses."

"Jason, Jackson, get over here," Bart yelled. "We got work to be do'n."

CHAPTER TEN

Bart leveled his sights on the paper target 70 feet distant. He had sat out the first round of shooting so he could get a perspective of "how this here thing is done." The man from Davisville had shot in the first round, but lost to Seth. Bart was certain, as most others, the contest would between that Davisville man and Seth for the prize gun. Cedric Oliver was officiating.

Prior to the first shoot, Cedric assigned each contestant a number which corresponded to a position across the field from a post. He announced the shooter's name, city of origin, type of shotgun, and whatever shooting titles the entrant may have to his credit. He got the information from the registration station which was run by Cyrus. There were eight of them in the first shoot, which took some time to say all that needed to be said about each. A few people clapped or shouted some encouragement to their favorite contestant.

The feller from Davisville had won more shooting titles than all the others combined. Cedric abbreviated most of them by saying "and a lot more," else they'd be there all day listening to the feller's shooting pedigree. His name was Williamson, and why he wanted to come shoot at this insignificant church organ fund-raiser was a mystery. One of the women folks, selling cups of hot coffee and cake slices, said something from the Bible which made sense about him being a hero everywhere but in his own home. He may be out to cure his local ignominy.

Mr. Williamson didn't look any more special than all the other folk. He fit right in with his coveralls and fine fedora hat. He didn't have medals hanging off his chest or patches sewed all over his coveralls. He seemed to be a regular fellow, not any taller and not a squatty body. He could get lost in a crowd, and you couldn't pick him out from ten other look-a-likes. People talked with him just like he was one of their own kin, not some kind of national celebrity. Naw, he wasn't snooty and full of himself. The way he figured it: if he won, he won; if he lost, he lost.

There were a bunch of youngsters like Jason and Jackson who thought they could best him of the honor of being the winner. But, in their youthful exuberance and naivete, they may not have given any consideration to his years of being an expert veteran shooter. Besides, they would exhaust their fifty-cent pieces in a hurry buying sweets from all the girls. They were the real competition, not those little paper targets or Mr. Williamson. Oblivious to the real purpose of having the turkey shoot, they gave the shooting a try all the same. Wouldn't it have been something if one of those upstarts had won! Lordy, their feet wouldn't have touched the ground for a month. Their heads would be swollen full of themselves like a harvest moon.

Eugenia stayed mostly at a table selling bedcovers her mother had stitched. She had some wonderful patterns of patched cloth. Most all the ladies admired her mother's talent with a needle. They asked about her mother's health and remarked that they wanted to visit soon one Sunday afternoon following church. The customary visiting hours to receive guests was between the noon meal and supper. If one came before or after, they were expected to be invited to a meal or bring their own basket. Around 4:00 P.M. a snack of cookies, and maybe a glass of home brew wine or beer, would be served depending on the time of year and the weather conditions.

Bart's old smooth-bore was loaded with rat shot. He had received special dispensation from the committee of Cedric and Cyrus on the nature of his shell. It was a center-fire like a shotgun, but the caliber was not the same gauge. Mr. Williamson looked over the rifle to satisfy himself the Remington would take the smokeless powder. He didn't want Bart's rifle to explode and send shards of metal flying all over the place.

Cedric and Cyrus stood by until Mr. Williams gave his 'Okay'. Mr. Williams remarked, "There should be separate divisions for rifle and shotguns. But it don't matter, let the boy shoot." He said something about Damascus and twist steel barrels that none seemed to understand but the three of them.

Eugenia had her hands folded under her chin as she watched. She closed her eyes for a flicker of a moment to send a prayer skyward. She unclasped her hands and covered her ears. When the first round was shot, she jumped and banged her knees on the table. They throbbed.

Bart could see a puff of wood dust rise from under his target. One of Cedric's little helpers retrieved the spent targets and snapped another into the bite of the clothes pin attached to the post. He brought the numbered targets to Cedric. The committee decided Mr. Williamson had the most pellet holes within the confines of the target ring. That made one win for Seth, one for Williamson, and none for Bart.

Since Williamson was shooting in all the matches, Bart could not ask to borrow his shotgun unless he sat out a match. "You might aim just a little above the target," Mr. Williams suggested to Bart.

"Thanks. I guess I'm more used to shootin' at chicken weasels than a piece of paper. That shore is a purty piece of fireworks you got there, sir. I never seen nuthin' like it, no sir, never before. Is that real gold all etched in there?"

Mr. Williamson turned the stock and looked, "I suppose so. Won this over at the state fair in Raleigh last year. It's all hand-tooled by a master gunsmith. You ought to get the feel of it. Here, take a hold to it."

Bart looked at Mr. Williams, "You sure you want me touchin' your gun."

"Go ahead. You won't bruise it, and it sure won't bite you."

"Gosh, it's so light. I thought it would be much heavier than this." Bart placed the stock into the shoulder cup and aimed down range. "Oh, this feels like it was made to order. If I had somethin' like this, I'd shoot out the center of all dem targets. You must be playin' with us only gettin' a few pellets through the paper."

"Would you like to shoot it next round? We could swap. You shoot mine, and I'll shoot yours."

"You don't mean that. You're pullin' my leg. You want to shoot this old thing?"

"It's been a while. Reminds me of the first rifle I had as a youngster. I could knock a squirrel out of the top of a walnut tree with mine. You don't mind if I give it a try?"

"I'm getting the better part of the swap. Let me run over there and give 'em another registration payment. Don't you go nowheres. I'll be right back."

Bart ran to Seth's registration table. "Mr. Boyd, listen here, Mr. Williamson is going to let me shoot his fancy shotgun. I didn't even ask." Cyrus handed Bart a shell and assigned a target station.

Bart turned and was about to run back, "Oh, Bart?"

"Yes, sir."

"Good luck."

"Thank you. I won't need it with this shotgun. I'm going to blow a hole out of that paper target."

Eugenia saw Bart swap his rifle for Mr. Williamson's shotgun. Bart handed him a rat-shot cartridge from his pocket. She stood up and winced from the contusion on her knees. Her hands were folded under her chin as before. Her eyes closed in prayer as the men and boys stepped forward and loaded their shells into the chambers. "Oh, please, Lord. You know I don't ask for much very often, but this is special. Please, let my Bart hit the target this time." She opened her eyes and kept her hands folded under her chin. She clutched a cross on a chain around her neck for good luck.

"Remember, it aims low," Bart whispered to Mr. Williamson.

"Right," he responded. "That shotgun has a bit more kick than your rifle. Just hold her tight and steady."

"I ain't never fired a shotgun before," Bart returned.

"Well, let's do it."

When the smoke cleared, Bart ejected the spent shell from the chamber and left the breach open. He handed the shotgun back to Mr. Williamson. "That was shore a treat. You 'bout the nicest gentleman I ever met to let me fire off with. I sorta hope you win this day."

Cedric took the targets over to Cyrus. They conversed and passed the targets back and forth between themselves.

"There is a tie between Mr. Williamson and Mr. Rombert. Therefore, a second shooting between the two will determine the winner." Mr. Williamson was handed a fresh shell by Mr. Oliver. Bart had never been addressed as "Mr. Rombert" in his entire life. He naturally assumed Cedric was calling another's name from the file of shooters. He had been called "Mister Bart" by Jason and Jackson, and Bart by all others all his life. Hearing "Mr. Rombert" summoned nothing familiar in him but a distant memory of a deceased relative.

"That shore was a pleasure, Mr. Williamson. She fires a smooth shot and handles like nothin' I ever helt afore. I thank 'e fer givin' me 'sperience I never had afore now. She shore is a sweet one."

"Well, you are mighty nice. Better load up. You and I are in a shoot-off tie."

"We are?"

"Your last name Rombert?"

"Yes sir, it is."

"Is there another one in the match?"

"No sir. I'm the only one in these parts."

"You meaning to tell me, the two of us shot the same?"

"That's what the judge called."

"Well, I'll be."

"Remember. She shoots low. Aim at the top of the target."

"Yes, sir. I shore will."

Bart pulled another cartridge from his pocket and slid it into the rifle chamber. "I feel kinda nervous standing here just the two of us with everybody watching."

"Good luck, son."

"Thank you. Same to you."

Eugenia went through her ritual.

When the smoke cleared, the targets were retrieved.

Rat shot in a rifle shell has only half the number of pellets of a 12-gauge shotgun shell. The odds are overwhelmingly in Mr. Williamson's favor. The side betting favored Mr. Williamson three to one for this reason alone. His experience and reputation counted heavily as well. The odds went to five to one which means if you bet a dime, you got back a fifty-cent piece. Ed Watson was holding the bet money and keeping book.

More people were tense about the outcome than Bart and Williamson from Davisville. They may have betted on Williamson, but they were cheering for Bart, especially Eugenia. She didn't give a flip about the prize shotgun or the turkey and ham. She wanted her beau to stand out and be noticed. She wanted to be holding his left hand when everybody was congratulating him and shaking his right hand. She wanted to share all his back slaps from the church elders on being such a good marksman. Her pride and vanity were at stake. She almost wished that Bart hadn't entered the contest. What if he should lose? She would be linked to a person that others would consider to be a loser.

When the tabulation was taken, both had the same number of pellet holes through the target paper. However, Bart had one addition pellet hole on the outer edge of the black target circle. Cedric and Cyrus studied the targets and claimed Bart to be the winner fair and square. He could have his choice of a ham or turkey as a prize. He took a salt-rubbed smoked ham, claiming he was going to learn how to make biscuits to eat along with the meat. He got a kiss on the cheek from Eugenia.

Bart shook Mr. Williamson's hand and told him what a pleasure it was to be matched up against an expert such as himself. Ed Watson was as happy as a crow on collecting nearly twenty dollars in bets he didn't have to pay off. After the shoot was over, he gave Bart a ten-dollar gold certificate out of his winnings. Bart thought on that bill and how he got it. He turned around and gave the ten-dollar gold certificate to Mr. Oliver as a donation to the organ fund, claiming he had all the satisfaction a man could receive by being called Mr. Rombert and besting Mr. Williamson from Davisville in a tie-breaker shoot-off.

Bart retired from shooting after the match because he had fired the only three rat-shot cartridges he had. All his ammunition was gone. Seth offered him his shotgun, but Bart refused saying, "I had better quit while I'm ahead." Seth got back into shooting targets, but Mr. Williamson took the day and the grand prize.

Mr. Williamson called Bart, "I heard about your giving the bet winnings to the church organ fund."

"Yes, sir. I thought the money was ill got."

"Tell you what I'd like to do. I admire a lad that's got principles. I want you to have the shotgun I won here today. I got more of them than I know what to do with as it is. I only really shoot for sport anyways. Today, you gave me more than the gun's worth. I almost forgot what this was all about. I'd truly like to give you back something in return."

"I can't take that shotgun. It's worth a month's pay. I didn't earn it no how."

"I want to make a gift of it to you."

"No sir. You won that fair and square."

"Tell you what then. Will you take the old one from the state fair? I'll keep this one to remember this day by. I know you admired it."

"I ain't never had a present like this in my whole life."

"Now you got to make a promise to me."

"What's that?"

"With this shotgun and the way you shoot, you got to promise me you won't go on tour around the country and shoot against me ever again. I know when I'm beat. If you had more shells for that weasel rifle, you would have won the shotgun yourself. I have no doubt about that, son."

"I guess that promise would be something of value to trade."

"A man's word is as good as gold."

"Let's call it a done deal then," Williamson said.

All her mother's quilts sold that day. Two ladies were actually arguing over one especially nice work and ended up paying double the asking price. One of the two women was Azalee Palmer, Seth's wife.

Years later, long after she and Bart were married, she would repeat with swollen pride the turkey shoot story at the church camp meeting while perched in the porch swing, her knitting in hand. Once the turkey shoot was over, everybody disbursed hither and yon to clean up and change into their finest dance clothes. It was a day Bart would never forget.

CHAPTER ELEVEN

There wasn't a building large enough in Butler to hold a dance. The Elmer Municipal Center, the largest building in the county, was reserved. Generally, officials didn't approve of churches mixing in with politics for fear that politics would get mixed in with religion. Preachers and politicians naturally didn't trust one another. Each had a divergent point of view when it came to interpreting the Gospel and the Constitution.

In Cedric's petition before the county commissioners, of which he was one, he stressed that other non-government groups had used the facility. He named the Democratic party, the Klan, and the Boy Scouts as organizations that had held rallies on the premises. "Why should other worthwhile groups be excluded from having the use of a public facility?" he asked. "This is nothing more than a dance. There will be no alcoholic beverages in the building other than what you may sneak in on your own. I suspect all of us will be there shaking the hands of our constituents." The petition was approved without assessing a charge to the Baptist church sponsors.

Eugenia and her mother had been cutting fabric and stitching for weeks. Eugenia mail-ordered triple-crinoline pet-ticoats to boost out her skirt and six yards of lace to starch and sew. At Eugenia's suggestion, Bart visited Aaron Cohen.

Stella Cohen asked Bart if he needed help. "Uh, is Mr. Cohen available?"

"Yes sir, what may I do for you this fine day?" Aaron enthusiastically asked.

"Have you heard of the dance coming up?" Bart asked.

"Why sure. Half the town has been in here to purchase festive clothes for the splendid occasion. Do you know your sizes?"

"I thought I would sell you an advanced ticket."

"Young man. I'm most sorry to admit, but I have already purchased tickets for myself and my wife. I'm pleased to know that you will be there. I look forward to seeing you. Have you thought about what you are going to wear?"

"Uh, I might need a shirt and slacks. I have a nice suit, but Eugenia tells me that I need something more casual, but dressy. I think those were her words."

"Please, allow me to show you a few shirts from which the other men have selected. Right this way. These are the Bob Wills style of shirt. Notice the mother-of-pearl snap buttons and the fine weave of the fabric and the double stitching in the seams. With your blue eyes and blond hair, I would suggest this light plaid."

"I'll take it. How much is it?" Bart asked.

"Only two dollars."

"Um, that's a lot for a shirt I might only wear one time."

"If you purchase a pair of slacks to match the shirt, I'll drop the price to $1.50. How does that sound?"

"Better. I don't want no plaid pants though. How much are the slacks?"

"Oh, it depends on your size and the style. Follow me, please."

"Would you be offended if I measure your waist and in-seam?"

"No sir, I've never been measured before. I just buy medium size at Palmer's."

"I can tell. They only have three men's sizes: small, medium and large."

"I can clearly see you are not a small or a large. Do you prefer a snug fit to accentuate your manliness?"

"I ain't sure what you are talkin' 'bout."

"Do you dress from the right or the left?"

"I usually put my right leg in first."

"That is interesting but not quite the answer that I'm

looking for. Is the angle of your dangle more often on the right leg or the left?"

"Excuse me? Are you asking what I think you're asking?"

"Precisely so. Do you wear undergarments?"

"No. And Mr. Cohen, they just fall where they go. It don't matter none to me at all. I ain't 'tickler about none of that."

After Cohen took a waist measurement, he asked, "Would you like to try these on for comfort and fit? The men's dressing room is behind the red curtain, there on the back right."

When Bart returned, he said to Aaron, "I think these pants were made for a giant. I'll have to get me a pair of stilts."

"Oh, Mr... , what did you say your name was?"

"Bart."

"Your full name, please."

"Bartholomew Rombert."

"Do you prefer to be addressed as Mr. Rombert or as Bartholomew Rombert, Esquire?"

"Golly, you ask a bunch of questions. Bart will do fine. Thank 'e kindly."

"If you favor this pair of slacks, we can have them hemmed to your length. Will they be with or without a cuff?"

"I ain't got a notion what you're talkin' 'bout, Mr. Cohen. Maybe you best show me the difference betwixt 'em."

"The slacks I am wearing have a dress cuff. One without a cuff will simply have the fabric turned under. With these slacks and for dancing, I would recommend no cuff. Will that be acceptable?"

"Sure, fine."

"Would you care to browse in footwear? Perhaps a belt?"

"What's the whole shooting match going to run? I don't know if I have all this much money."

"We would be happy to place you on the installment plan," Aaron Cohen suggested.

"What's that?"

"Oh, you pay a little each week or month that suits your budget. Fifty cents a week or two dollars a month."

"Okay let's go for the shirt, pants, belt, and footwear for fifty cents a week."

"It is such a pleasure working with you Mr. Bart. Mrs. Cohen will have you sign for the charges. Thank you, and have a most pleasant day."

"Do I take all the stuff with me, or do I come back after it's all paid off?"

"Oh, by all means, Mr. Bart, you will have the use of the clothing immediately. Only a few minutes are necessary to cut and hem the pants. Do you mind waiting?"

"No sir. I heard a lot about your crapper. May I have a viewin' whilst I'd be here?"

"My pleasure. Right this way, please."

No European man who gets talked about takes to hoedown dancing right off the bat. Dancing is as strange for a country man as it would be for a horse. Both have to be taught how to shuffle their legs by someone else. About all Bart had seen of dancing was when a troupe of minstrels set up in front of Palmer's and began to make noise with a banjo, spoons, harmonica, and a washboard. The performer playing the washboard had sewing thimbles on several of his fingers, which made the sound coming off that board, in Bart's opinion, even worse.

Seth ran them off his porch right off. He said they were scaring his customers away. Two youngsters were shuffling their feet and slapping their chests, hands, and thighs in synchronization to the music. They seemed to have a beat all their own. All of them were begging money. The one on the banjo had a gold front tooth, the first Bart had ever seen.

When Bart heard there was going to be a dance, the gyrating he had seen at Palmer's was his mental image of what dancing was all about. He told Eugenia so when she asked if he could dance. He said that he had seen it before at Palmer's and, if them jungle heathens could do it, so could he. He asked her if dancing was wicked because what he had seen was more like a St. Vitus dance of the devil than something that was spiritual.

She asked him one evening when the subject reared its ugly head again about dancing. She asked him to give her a demonstration.

"You mean right here in front of everybody?" Bart asked.

"Now is as good a time as any. Besides, in a couple of hours the band is going to be playing, and I'd rather know now what kind of dance partner I've got, than to find out later," Eugenia answered.

"There ain't no music a'playin'. A man can't dance without no music," he pleaded as an excuse.

"We've got the radio right here. I'll get you a tune."

"This ain't necessary for ever'un to be watchin.'"

"Soon, Eugenia tuned in a Paul Whiteman foxtrot being broadcast from Chicago and transmitted by local stations to the kitchen Brunswick Radiola."

"Okay," Cyrus and Martha commanded. "Let's see what you've got." They pulled up their ladder-back chairs.

"I'd rather turn around to where I don't have to face you. This is just foolishness. Why can't we just sit and watch the others do the dancing?" he pleaded.

"Nope. A civilized man has to dance," Martha said firmly, "especially on his wedding night. Cyrus did it. And you're gonna have to do the same."

"It's a whole lot better with just the three of us watching than a whole room full of people," Eugenia said.

"I don't see a whole a lot of difference one way or t'other. It's all about the same to me. You got to promise you won't laugh."

"We all promise," Eugenia said as she crossed her heart.

"Cyrus, why don't you get out there with him to keep him company?" Martha asked.

"Oh, Lordy. Martha you know my knee took lame the other day and will hardly work. I best stay off it so it will be healed and be fresh for this evening."

"Okay, on the count of three. One. Two. Three. Go!" Eugenia said.

"You're counting too fast. I wasn't ready," Bart said.

"This ain't like jumping off a rock at the swimming hole. You just start when the next tune is played. That will be your cue to begin," Cyrus prompted. "You got to get your ears wet sooner or later."

"Y`all really gonna make me do this?" Bart begged Eugenia.

"Yep." Cyrus answered. "It's part of the passage from boyhood to manhood. We all got to go through with the suffering to please the womenfolk. We may not like it. We may not enjoy it. But we gotta do it, or else they will shame us for the rest of our natural-born lives."

"Okay, Dad, that is about enough. You're going to scare him back to his holler, and he'll never come out. Let me do the talking," Eugenia said.

Bart rolled his eyes in a big loop. He didn't like what he saw when those minstrels were jumping all about, and he hated the thought of imitating their antics. "All right here goes nuttin'. Don't laugh now."

"We won't. I promise," Eugenia affirmed. She licked her fingers and pointed to the sky.

"Honest Ingun?" Bart childishly asked.

When the tune started, Bart began to jump around slapping his chest, hands, and thighs. He shuffled his feet without any concept of keeping a beat with the music. Cyrus could not hold himself back any longer. "He… he …looks… like he has bees in his drawers." Cyrus punctuated nearly all his words with loud laughing to the point that he fell out of his chair and rolled over on his back. Martha couldn't hold her giggles either. She was kind enough to cover her mouth, but her shoulders were rolling, and her eyes were tearing.

"Slapping at the bees… in his drawers," Cyrus bellowed from the floor. He laughed so violently he could hardly catch his breath. His sides were aching in pain. "Bees… in his… drawers," Cyrus managed to get out. "Slapping… at the… bees."

Tears poured from his eyes. His body wriggled and shook with uncontrollable levity.

"Stop!" yelled Eugenia. "You call that dancing?"

"Well, that's what I seen done up at Palmer's. They was collectin' pennies."

She up-righted Cyrus' chair. With a deep sigh, she said, "Lord have mercy on our souls, Bartholomew Rombert."

"I'm glad we had a chance to see your dance early because it sure would have caused a commotion in the city," Cyrus said from the floor. He wiped his eyes. "Do it again."

Eugenia whipped around. "Daddy!" Turning back to Bart, she cordially smiled, "Now, Bart, your dance was just fine. We only have to adjust a couple of things."

"Like shaking the bees out of his drawers," Cyrus quipped. He fell back to the floor and began his bellowing laugh again.

Martha had to get up and leave the side porch. Cyrus' laugh was setting her off into another spasm of giggles. She couldn't contain them.

Eugenia's face was stern. They had promised not to laugh and had turned on their word. She was not pleased with her father's behavior far more than the displeasure from Bart's silly dance.

"Forget what you just did. That wasn't dancing. Not at all. Dad, you can get up and go into the house with mother. I'll deal with Bart's dancing lessons." Looking back at Bart, "Now, the first thing is to tap your foot to the beat of the music. Watch me."

"You gotta do it, Son, or they will be shaming you for the rest of your life," Cyrus stiffly remarked as he was leaving the side porch. He didn't like being ordered about by his daughter, but he would give her room on the dancing business.

"Do as I do," she instructed. "Okay, fine. Now, put your hand at my waistline here on the side. Next, we hold hands out here like you're reaching to get something from the closet shelf. We keep about six inches apart so our bodies don't touch. When you take a step forward, I take a step backwards. Forget all that jiggling. Keep your hands where I put them. Don't do any slapping. We are going to do it respectable-like. Not like those minstrels you saw. You just get them out of your mind like you never saw them."

"This isn't so bad," Bart enthusiastically announced. "I'd rather hang onto you anyhow."

"Okay, start forward."

"Oops. Sorry. I didn't mean to tromp of your shoe."

"Take smaller steps."

"I never walked with nobody this way before."

"This is called the dancing walk. We're not over yet. We don't look at each other. You watch where you are going so you don't bump into another dance couple."

"There ain't nobody here but us two."

"Just pretend we are on the floor at the dance. I watch behind you so no one will dance into us. You never know if the dance floor will be crowded with a whole bunch of people."

"Okay."

"Now, stop taking steps forward, or we'll be down yonder in the pond. Take some backward steps and get the feel of that."

"Good. Now, I want to show you how to swing your partner and doe-see-doe, that's really the best part of dancing."

"I think I'm going to like this a whole lot."

"Don't forget to smile at everyone that's looking at us like we are having the best time of our lives. When you feel comfortable with the walking, you can smile at me too like you would rather be dancing with me than any other girl."

"Well, I am. You don't have to tell me that. I've got no eyes for nobody but you."

"There might be some flirts there. You be careful not to encourage them. Let me do all the talking unless we get visited by a man. You can talk to all them you want to. I won't get jealous."

"You'd get jealous if I talked to a flirt?"

"I'd slap your face in a heartbeat."

"How about talkin' to old widowed women or children?

They safe to talk with?"

"You let me be the judge of that. This is about all we can do here. It's about time to get washed and change. You can dress with Dad. Mother will come to my room to dress. Mind your manners."

"I'm gonna stick close by you so's you'll get me through this ordeal."

"You never know. You might enjoy it."

As Martha and Cyrus took their seats in the kitchen, Martha said, "Cyrus, I'm not all that sure about Bart and Eugenia."

Cyrus was jolted by her comment. "He's mighty found of her, and he's a good worker. I don't see what more a girl could ask for."

"I think he's wounded by the loss of his family. I'm concerned his wound is festered and he is in emotional pain."

"He seems ordinary to me. He never mentions anything about being in pain. I'm around him most all the time, and I never hear him talk about suffering emotional wounds. I think I ought to know."

"That's what bothers me. He doesn't talk about it. I think it is all bottled up inside of him, building steam, and ready to explode."

"I never seen him lose a temper or even get much rattled by things. If anything, I think he's mellow. I know a person never really gets over the loss of their parents, but he doesn't seem to carry it as a burden."

"I guess what I'm thinking about is his attaching himself to Eugenia and us as his surrogate family. We are his missing parents, and Eugenia is the only love in his life. If he had more experience with girls or if he came from a big family that had lots of relations, I think he wouldn't be so vulnerable. To Bart, the world revolves around our daughter. What if they had words between them?"

"There is no telling what he might do. Passion is the most wicked of weapons. It makes sane men crazy. I just think he might need some counseling advice on handling his grief. He was just a fragile boy when he was orphaned. I don't want, and I know you feel the same way if you ponder on him, Eugenia to become a victim of a love sick boy. You know how fickle girls can be. What if she changes her mind all of a sudden? What then?"

"If you have something particular in mind, why don't you have a little chat with him. Maybe you are making a mountain out of a mole hill."

Eugenia came into the house while Bart fetched his dancing clothes from the wagon. Eugenia stepped out onto the porch. "Bart, can I have a private word with you?" she asked.

"Yes'um."

"I just thought you might like a little advice on matters."

"Yes, ma'am."

"I thought I would speak to you on matters of love."

"Yes'um. Go right ahead."

"A young man, one without much experience at the art of love, might need a little help from time to time. Now, he might not know he needs help but sometimes it can be obvious to everyone but him. Do you know what I mean?"

"Yes'um. They say the last thing a fish learns about is the difference between water and air."

"That may be true if we were fishing. The fish naturally wants to get back into the water… but I don't think I had fish in mind or for that matter air and water either. I do have in mind differences between boys and girls and how they look at love."

"Yes'um. I'm sorry about saying what I did about fish. That was just the first thing that popped up in my mind."

"That's quite all right. You're a bright young man, and a little bit of insight can go a long way with you. Some things do and don't apply to all situations. I wanted to give you something to think about that you can apply with Eugenia. I'm telling you from a woman's point of view, so Cyrus would want to argue on it, but he's not listening."

"Yes'um. I don't really understand what you're saying."

"Let me start at this again. In Greek mythology, Venus, the goddess of love, commanded her son, Cupid to make people fall in love. Most think Cupid is a fat little cherub that flies around on little baby-feathered wings with a miniature bow and arrow. Two people fall in love when they are smitten by his arrow shot into their hearts. I thought you might like to know this isn't true. It's all made up to help people explain what they feel but can't see."

"I never knew about it in the first place. So if'n you're telling me a lie that I ain't never heard of ain't true …"

"No, no, no," Martha interrupted. I didn't mean that either. She scratched her head. She had Bart's undivided attention.

"Yes'um."

"Okay, here goes straight out. Boys love what they see with their eyes. Girl's love because of what they hear with their ears. You love Eugenia because she is a handsome figure of a girl. She wants to love you because of the sweet little nothings you say to her. Every girl loves to hear sweet things about the hundred ways you love her. When you do this, she becomes more beautiful in your eyes. One feeds the other. Tonight, when you are together, try to think of ten different ways to tell her how much you love her. Most importantly, don't compare her to any other girl. If you do what I say, she will be yours forever. They call it wooing. Every day your love will grow, as will hers."

"Yes'um. I need some practice awful bad at getting my thoughts connected up to the words."

"You'll know when she likes what you are saying. You'll know when she doesn't too. Have you ever listened to the birds chirping to one another?"

"Oh, yes ma'am. I sure have."

"The male with the best song wins the hen."

"So, that's what the fuss is all about. I thought they were just happy."

"Go practice on that mule of yours. I'll bet she works better when you aren't mad at her. I'll bet she works better when you stroke her neck and whisper in her ear with a sweet loving voice. Try singing her a song and watch her ears perk up."

"How'd you know that?"

"I've been around mules and girls, and they are all about the same."

"I never thought about Eugenia being like a mule."

"Believe me, they both like sugar better than the whip."

"How'd you do?" Cyrus asked.

"I sent him down to the barn to talk to his mule. I'm not sure I made any sense to him."

"I could have told you that. He'll get more out of the mule than he ever could from you," Cyrus chided.

"I'd like to see you do any better," Martha bit back.

"That boy is so plumb in love, I think you'd be better off talking with Eugenia."

"There's not time before we have to get dressed and get on our way. Besides, I don't think there's an urgency. I'll chew on it a spell. When the time comes, we'll have our ladies' chat."

"Y'all should have had it long ago."

"There wasn't a point to it. She just got this beau. It came on all of a sudden like. He went from a millhand to a fiancée in a month."

"Bart asked me for Eugenia's hand the second day of work."

"What! And you never said anything to me?"

"I just thought it was their own business. Nobody interfered with you and me courting."

"I'm not interfering. I'm advising."

"You're meddling, no two ways about it."

"I don't want anybody to get their feelings hurt."

"They're loving each other. There ain't no pain to it."

"Hush. They might hear us talking about them."

"I don't mean to be the one that gets the last word in, but I feel like if they don't get along, then is the time to give them sympathy. Personally, I pray that time never comes. Eugenia and that boy are meant to be together just as much of God's will as for the two of us."

Martha came to Cyrus and put her hand on his cheek. "And I still love you as much today as I did the day I first set eyes on you."

Cyrus took her hand and kissed her palm. He stood and wrapped his arms around her. "And for what God has joined together, let no man or woman put asunder."

"It ain't written that way in the Bible."

"It ought to be."

CHAPTER TWELVE

Eugenia twisted and pinned her mother's hair on the top of her head. She pushed a gardenia into the bun. She plucked errant hair from her eyebrows, giving them greater shape. She rubbed black carbon from a burnt cork to cover over the grey. Eugenia plucked hairs from above Martha's upper lip, then spread red lip balm on both lips to make them full and appealing. Eugenia wanted her mother to look young and pretty again. She took a hot poker and twisted a locket of hair beside both of her mother's ears until they held a curl. When Martha viewed herself in the looking glass, she remarked at how "Sheik" Eugenia had made her appear. Martha put on a pair of dangling pearl earrings.

Martha hadn't been out in the public to affront the ladies for quite a spell. She never did care much for people, especially other women. She claimed, as did Cyrus, you couldn't tell what was on their minds. They would say one thing, then turn around and do another. Most all her family had died or moved far off, so she never had relatives to frequently visit or receive. Her sisters came to her wedding many years ago but hadn't visited since. Martha and Bart were the same in that respect. They had to count on themselves and nobody else.

Martha was a good reader. She was a member of the book-of-the-month club and received regular readings. She had just finished reading *Billy Budd, Foretopman* by Herman Melville and was about to start *The Magic Mountain* by Thomas Mann. She had segregated all of Joseph Conrad's books when he died as a memorial. They had their own place of reverence just like her collection of Emily Dickinson poems.

She had shelves full of books but never lended them. She

did once and never got the book back or another in return. She still held onto the grudge and would most likely take it to the grave with her. She had the only local 24-volume set of Encyclopedia Britannica besides the one at the county school house. She claimed to have read them from cover to cover, same with the 2,000 page Webster's International Dictionary.

She was self taught like Abraham Lincoln, but you would never know it. She kept her thoughts to herself unless you asked her a question straight out. She could spit out the answer quicker than you can snap your fingers. She would not go on and on like some do trying to impress you with knowledge. She had a natural inclination for learning because she enjoyed knowing all about people and places she would never see in Elmer county. That didn't mean she neglected her house, washing, or garden for the sake of reading books. She knew and kept her priorities in line.

She quit the churching mainly because she knew more about the Bible than the preacher or Sunday-school teachers. Listening to them get things all out of whack became disturbing. Then too, the women talked about trivialities that held no interest to her. They were self-absorbed in who they were, what they had, or who important they knew. She decided to sit home and read the Bible in solitude and contemplate the purity of Jesus on her own, without worrying if her dress was in style.

She made Cyrus proud. He was honored to be the husband of such a fine woman. He wished with a silent aching heart that he had more children, but that couldn't be helped. Eugenia was his miracle baby. He loved her as he did Martha, with all his heart and soul. When Bart came along, Cyrus found some satisfaction that seemed to complete the circle which he never realized was open. He thought he was all that Eugenia would ever need. He never gave a notion that she would come to love another. He consoled himself by thinking it was another kind of love, maybe the same kind that he felt for Bart himself. Then he changed his mind on that. It couldn't be the same. He thought about the way he loved his parents and his love for

Martha and came to the conclusion there were three kinds of love. He added a fourth. The love he had for milling.

Cyrus tried to figure the difference between love and like. There was the old mill dog that would roll his head from side to side and show his teeth every morning in a smile. Having only a stub for a tail, the smile was the only way the dog had to show he was happy to see Cyrus. A salesman once remarked the dog was a small Australian sheepdog variety, but no one could speculate on how the animal had found its way to the mill. There weren't Australians anywhere in the county, and nobody knew of one passing though.

The dog, regardless of his origin, would relentlessly pursue a rat until throttled and vigorously shaken to death. For this reason he was prized and rewarded with bits of ham scraps. He was named Dispatch. When Cyrus opened the mill, Dispatch would have his night's kill of rats lined up and beg for his reward. Cyrus liked the dog, but knew when the day came, he would have to bury him as though he were a member of the family.

When the four left for the church dance, they pulled up behind Seth and his family on the road. Cyrus blew his horn. "Hey Seth," Cyrus called, "You headed to the dance?"

He had a car packed full of children who swung around and waved. They yelled something different in chorus. Before long, Seth had a car in front of him, then another, till the line of cars ran over the hill and around the curve. Everybody was tooting horns and yelling to one another friendly greetings like at midnight on New Years Eve or such.

Eugenia coaxed Bart, Cyrus, and Martha into singing popular songs: "There's A Rainbow 'Round My Shoulder" by Al Jolson, "Sweet Georgia Brown" by Guy Lombardo and His Royal Canadians, "Comin' Thro' the Rye" like Marcella Sembrich. They sang a couple of country songs: "Papa's Billy Goat" by Fiddlin' John Carson, the old familiar "Comin' 'Round The Mountain," to which they had 'Gran'ma carrying Bart's bees and a sack of Boyd Flour in her wagon' and "On Top Old Smokey."

Bart had forgotten all about dancing. He was in another world, totally lost in the joy the experience brought. He had never been more happy in his life - being with the Boyds, doing what they were doing, and sitting next to Eugenia. The feeling was mutual, warm, and loving.

"Whoops. Looks like we got a flat tire," Cyrus announced. "We were almost there too." He pulled to the side of the road in a soft grassy spot. A couple of cars slowed down and asked if help was needed. "No problem. I've got a good spare. We'll have it fixed in a jiffy." To another he said, "Don't let that band start up without Bart there."

Bart realized what was ahead of him. His big blue eyes rolled around in their sockets. He less enthusiastically worked at the car jack. The more he thought about the dancing, the more his hands and feet took on a sweat. He thought about jumping into the cold creek to cool himself off. He knew what a trapped animal must feel like. He thought to himself, "Can't shake this loose. I'm shore enough caught. Ain't not a thing goin' to get me out of this here exceptin' that I fall flat dead on the spot."

"How's it going?" Eugenia asked.

All Bart's fears were swept away when he looked at her. "Have her fixed in no time."

"Don't forget to wash your hands when we get to the dance hall. I don't want that grease smeared all over my dress."

"Yes'um."

"You don't have to say 'Yes'um' to me," she rebutted. "I'm your sweetheart, not your mother."

"I forgot."

"Forgot! You forgot I'm your sweetheart," Eugenia chastised.

Martha leaned back over the seat, "Okay, you two. That's enough of that. It's nothing but nerves you got. Settle down and be nice."

"I'm sorry for yelling at you." Eugenia became coy.

"I'm sorry for saying 'Yes'um'. I meant to say, 'yes, my dear sweetheart.' It just got all tripped up and tangled on my tongue on the way out."

Eugenia gave Bart a smile that could have melted the tires off their steel rims. Her hair was up on her head like her mother's. Her neck was bare, and so was most of her chest and shoulders. He had never seen so much bare skin and bosom in his life. They were huge and pushed together with only a fine line of separation like when fat-boy Jackson bent over with his trousers hanging half down and his shirt pulled loose, shooting a moon with his fat ass. His heart was pounding; his eyes were starring lustfully. She looked so beautiful in her bare-topped new dancing dress. He wanted to haul her off into the woods like at the camp meeting and do something awful.

"There, all fixed. Y'all hang on whilst I drop the jack down. Do ya'hear?"

Cyrus cranked the car. The end of the line was out of sight. He turned the switch for the car lights.

Other than the lights at the movie house across from the parking lot, not many lights were brightened around the city hall. <u>The Thief of Baghdad</u> was playing staring Douglas Fairbanks. Bart had never been to a picture show and wondered what they were all about.

Small groups of men, segregated by age, were clustered in various places along the way through the parking lot to the hall opening. Some were chewing and spitting. Others were smoking. They passed a clear Mason jar of shine between themselves.

On seeing the jar being passed, Martha spoke to them, "You men know there's a prohibition on spirits."

Cyrus added, "Gentlemen, you might want to keep that Kerosene out of the ladies' sight."

Bart overheard one man saying, "Every time I have a drink too many, I get my boy, Malachi, to drive me home from the tavern. You'd be surprised how good a 13-year old can handle a car. Guess it's not no different from a tractor. But anyway, one night he asked me if I got drunk because I was afraid of his driving or because I couldn't drive because I was drunk. I take him every time I go to the tavern."

Another group was talking about the Harry Sinclair and Secretary Fall. One had bribed the other into issuing fraudulent oil leases on a Teapot Dome. They made no sense at all to Bart.

Another bunch was talking about the chances of the Washington Senators taking the pennant against the New York Yankees and getting to the World Series. One of the guys said something about Walter Johnson's arm holding out. Cyrus exchanged a friendly greeting with all of them.

Inside the doorway, young boys between ten and fourteen were smoking cigarettes and coughing on their own smoke. Martha scolded them, "Shame on you boys. When I see your mothers, I'm going to tell them what you're doing." She had no idea who the boys were, but they threw down their cigarettes and ran inside.

Each handed over their tickets to Cedric inside the door. He had a table with a lockbox where he kept the money from those who didn't buy tickets in advance. A stack of unsold tickets had a rubber band twisted around them. Another larger box held all the ticket stubs. Several would be pulled out for door-prize drawings during the band's intermissions.

Bart said, "I need to wash the grime off my hands from changin' that tire. I'll be right back."

"I'll walk with him to make sure he doesn't get lost."

"Eugenia," Martha called, "Your daddy and I will be sitting near the far left side. You look for us over there, Okay?"

"Yes, Momma."

"If you don't find us, then sit with the Palmer family. You hear?"

"Yes, Momma."

Finally, after a prolonged delay, Bart emerged from the men's room. There was talk about John W. Davis from West Virginia running against Calvin Coolidge. Nobody favored Coolidge since he was a Vermont Republican and a damned

Yankee liberal. All felt that he would restore the south's sacred honor. Bart had never voted and received advice on getting himself registered, much like the coaching from Cyrus.

"What took you so long? I've been standing here for a good ten minutes."

"They wanted to know how I was gonna vote. Hew-we, I never knew people could get so worked up over politics. You ought to go in there and listen to them men carry on."

"Thanks, but no thanks. I'd rather use the ladies' room. Why don't we try dancing?"

"Don't you want a swallow of water or something first?"

"I'm fine. Come on." Eugenia pulled at Bart's hand.

"I've got a better idea."

"What's that?"

"Let's just stand here for a spell and watch how the others are a doing the dancing. I could imitate so as not to stick out like a sore thumb and all."

"Just once. That's all. After that we are going to dance."

"Okay, my dear sweetheart."

The fiddler stopped swinging his bow as Sheriff Hothgart stepped onto the stage. He was an imposing man, not only in size, but in commanding respect with full uniform including his service revolver holstered at his side. The banjo player slowed his picking down to a stop.

"Ladies and gentlemen, may I have your attention." There was an uproar of disapproval. "Quiet please!" Folks settled down and faced him. The drummer did a little roll that caught the Sheriff's irritated attention. "I apologize for interrupting your dance. We'll get started back in just a minute or two. So, don't fret. I have a very important announcement to make, so if you would, listen up. My prisoner, Benny Parsons, has escaped out of the jail. You remember him; he is the one that stole the mail from Norma. Well, that is a federal offense, and we were holding him for the Federal Marshals to pick up. Seems that everybody at the jail house is here tonight and nobody was watching him. Somehow or other, he got the keys to his cell and just walked out the front door without nobody noticing. So, listen up, I'm deputizing all you men from 21 to 65 to be on the lookout for him. Prize money will be paid for his capture."

Someone from the crowd yelled, "How much?"

"The going rate is $50.00. But you got to bring him in."

"What's he look like?" another asked.

"Oh, he is a good size. Blond wavy hair, blue eyes, and a good set of teeth. Early twenties, I think 22. Right now, he was in jail house clothes. Thanks for your attention. I don't believe he's dangerous, but I would use caution. We see him as a desperate fugitive from the law. Oh, I need to see my regular officers and staff up here by the stage for a briefing."

"Gash, Sheriff, here I am. It's me, Benny Parsons. I didn't do no jail break escape. I ain't gone nowheres. I'm right here. They let me out to come to this here dance. I'll be back at the jail house after this here shindig is over with. I gave them at the jail my word on that."

Everybody let go a raucous laugh. The joke was at the sheriff's expense for not knowing of Benny's temporary release. His lawyer, Ezra Peterson called the district attorney, who called the federal judge, who granted a temporary recognizance bond for the night. Benny was released to the custody of Ezra, based solely on Ezra's good faith word to the judge.

"Well, I'll be hornswoggled. All right, I un-deputize each and every one of you. Benny Parsons, you had better be at the jail house no later than midnight. Ezra you had better be with him. I got some words for both of you, but I ain't going to use them here in public. Okay, let's get on with this dance."

The drummer gave another drum roll and hit the cymbals. Hothgart gave him a severe look of consternation for making his official duty appear to be nothing more than a Vaudeville comedy act. A lot of people applauded, as they would a stage performance of slapstick comedy, thus adding greater humiliation to the sheriff's embarrassment. Hothgart waved to the crowd as he stepped from the stage platform and took the unwanted kudos bravely.

After a minute or two of talking among themselves, the band started the tune back at the beginning. Eugenia pulled Bart onto the dance floor. He wasn't anything spectacular but held his ground. He did just like Eugenia taught, smile and all. He only stepped on her shoes three times and bumped a few couples on the back walk. Eugenia and the Boyds were pleased to see them make a nice showing as a couple.

"Mr. Cohen did a fine job of dressing you," Martha said to Bart. "You look smarter than any man on the dance floor."

"Thanky, ma'am. That dress you made for Eugenia is 'bout the purttiest I ever did see. You shore have a hand with a needle and thread, ma'am."

Cyrus and Martha had taken a slow waltz on the dance floor. Martha whispered, "Look at the way Mary Goddard hangs on her husband. She's all over him. She ought to be ashamed to bring bedroom manners into a ballroom. Look! She has her leg between his. Her dress is above her knees, and that blouse is off her shoulders."

"Maybe he likes her looking that way."

"I hope you don't think I'd ever be so scandalous to dress like that."

The band took an intermission. Martha had to sit through the story about the killing of a milk snake that kept sucking on a freshened cow. Cyrus got the undiluted story during intermission about the cockfight at the Horton's barn from Ed Watson. Cyrus didn't care much for the raising of fighting poultry. Ed emphasized the length of the spurs that had been clamped onto the roosters as "sharper than the slice-and-dice butcher's blade."

When the Goddards came to pay respects to Martha, Mary Goddard bent over to take her hand. Cyrus glimpsed down her blouse. Her breasts were copious. Martha knocked his knee with hers. Cyrus stood.

"You don't think I didn't notice you looking down her dress," Martha remarked to Cyrus.

"I think she wanted me to take a look. Why else would

she bend way down and wear a shirt that is wide open."

"You better behave, or you'll be doing the cooking around the house from now on."

When the band resumed their positions on the stage, Dancing Dan, as he was called, asked the leader to play something with a jazzy swing. He and Selma Hammond spun and twisted in movements that doubled the tempo of the band's beat. A few other young kids joined. Eugenia tapped her foot.

"That is the new way of dancing. They call it the 'Leap Year Hop.'" When the band finished the spunky tune, all the young couples clapped. The old folks were stoic as if frozen in time.

Around midnight the band stopped playing. Most of the older people and young children had left for home much earlier, as did the Boyds.

"I hope we don't have another flat on the way home," Cyrus said.

"Do you have a tire-patchin' kit and a pump with ya?" Bart asked.

"Yep."

"Well, don't you worry none. I know how to patch a blowed tire."

After they snuggled back into the back seat of Cyrus' car, Bart asked, "Eugenia, you ever been to a picture show?"

"Yes. I've been to several, but not in a long time. Dad used to carry me to town when he visited the pharmacy to get mother's medicine. He would let me go see a moving picture. That was back before they had sound. Some woman played the piano and I watched Chaplin. He was so funny. I would tell mother the whole thing when I got home."

"I'd like to see one myself someday. I also want to do some voting for that Davis Democrat feller they all talkin' 'bout."

Cyrus said, "All you have to do is show up on voting day. We'll go together. They have the property-tax ledgers at the voting place. You just tell them who you are."

CHAPTER THIRTEEN

Before the sermon the following morning, Cedric Oliver announced to the congregation, "Over $1,000 was raised yesterday. The turkey shoot brought in $250, and the dance brought in $750. Other money has not been turned in for refreshment and handicraft sales." He said, "With matching donations we are still a couple of hundred away from being able to pay for the organ. However, I am certain that donations in the offering plate in the next several months will account for the difference. So, I'm going to go ahead and get the organ on order unless there is disagreement." Cedric paused and looked around. "I'll keep you informed of the progress as news develops. May God bless each and every one of you who worked so hard to get the organ for this church. Thank you."

The Reverend Allston Henslowe sat in a guest chair at the altar behind the pulpit. He would not preach, only render a closing prayer. The church had issued a call to Reverend Homer Madison Jolly. Kids, being what they are, called him the Jolly Mad Reverend behind his back. He had a great sense of humor but failed to demonstrate any affectations of mental illness other than a propensity to imbibe a dram or two of spirits on special occasions. The Reverend Henslowe was aware of the gossip on Jolly's free-thinking sobriety posture and made frequent biblical reference to drunkenness during the discourse of his prayer which, for all practical purposes, was as lengthy as Jolly's sermon on an entirely divergent subject. Due to his loquacious voracity, church was dismissed quite late.

Ed Watson fingered a few discordant notes during the final hymn "Lord, Dismiss Us with Thy Blessing." To make his performance even worse, he somehow lost his timing and was either behind or ahead of the congregational singing.

"Who's going to play the pipe organ when it gets here?" Eugenia asked her father.

"I hope not Ed, that's for sure."

Ed had learned bugling while serving with the Fourth U.S. Army Corps during the invasion of Hattonchatel, France, in September of 1918. After he lost nearly all of his front teeth in a German beer-hall fight, he took up the accordion. He figured he wouldn't lose all his fingers. Actually, he took the accordion from the beer hall and carried it with him for the duration of the war. In Ed's way of thinking, the accordion took him up. For his lack of talent, the church organ fund had been established. He had a big heart and brought music where there had been none.

When Cyrus, Eugenia, and Bart returned home from church, the kitchen was not filled with the usual warm smells of Martha's food. The Radiola was tuned to a religious station. The choir was singing "For All the Saints Who from Their Labors Rest." Martha was sedately sitting in her chair with sewing in her lap. Her glasses hung from her nose. Her fingers seemed frozen between stitches as though she were contemplating some deep thought that would take a while to resolve in her mind. "Honey, are you all right?" Cyrus asked. He had thought she had dozed off and lost track of the time of day. She had never been late with a Sunday dinner.

"She hadn't even started the biscuits," Eugenia thought.

As he walked closer, he realized her eyes were full open but not answering. "Honey?" Cyrus lifted her hand. The silver needle fell from her grip. She was cold. Her face had lost color. He felt her wrist for a pulse. There was none. "Eugenia," he called, "I think you better step over here. It's your mother."

With those few words, Eugenia's youth was swept away forever. Cyrus fell to his knees sobbing. "She danced with me last night." His tear-streaked face looked up at Eugenia. We talked about it last night as we prepared for bed. She said it was one of the happiest nights of her life. "Oh Eugenia, what am I gonna do without her. She was everything."

Bart walked into the room with a sense of knowing these moments should be private between father and daughter. He backed away and put on a pot of coffee. His way was different. He poured the grinds straight into the water and filtered the boiled result with a cheese cloth laid over a mug. He knew from experience with handling the dead, a lot of strong coffee would be needed in the days ahead. Bart stopped and cleared his throat, "I'll go get the preacher."

"No, wait a second, Bart. Help me lift her to her bed," Cyrus asked solemnly.

Eugenia gently lifted the sewing from her mother's lap as though she didn't want to disturb her sleep. She couldn't touch her, not yet, not even to pull her lids over her eyes. She could not force herself to place her mother's shoes back onto her feet which rested on a footstool beside her chair. She picked up the shoes and cuddled them to her breast as though she were keeping a kitten warm and secure.

Cyrus pushed her reading glasses up the bridge on her nose. They always slid down; she was always pushing them back up. The glasses were part of her ritual behavior. They slid their arms around her back and under her knees and laid her on the bed. Cyrus closed her eyes, dripping his tears onto her face. He pulled a handkerchief and wiped his face then hers. He pushed back a few errant hairs from her face and folded her hands on her chest. He kissed her lips.

Eugenia slid the shoes back on her mother's feet, then realized how scuffed and tattered they looked. The shoes were her mother's everyday house shoes. They were shabby. Eugenia wondered why she had never noticed them before. She realized how little her mother demanded for herself. She reflected on how much she had taken her mother for granted. How she always depended on her to always be there with a kind smile and a reassuring word. She realized that her mother always listened to her complaints and gave none of her own in return. She wondered if her mother knew the end was near and had gone to the dance as her last public outing, her farewell.

Eugenia fell on the bed and gripped her mother's waist. "Daddy, I'm going to miss her so much."

"A daughter has only one mother. You were all she needed."

"I wish she had on the dress she wore last night. That's the way I want to remember her - happy, gay, pretty, and trying to set the world aright."

"When the ladies get here, ask them to change her. You lay out Martha's things for them. This is about all we can do for right now until the preacher gets here."

"I'd better go fetch him," Bart said.

With tears again in his eyes, Cyrus said, "She loved you like you were her own son, Bart."

Bart's head dropped.

"She wasn't the kind of woman to parade her emotions all over the place. But she loved you like you were family. Get the preacher."

Bart reluctantly pulled himself away. He glanced at Eugenia, but she was absorbed in grief and did not see him. His heart was shredded not only for not giving Martha the recognition her love deserved but also in sympathy for Cyrus and Eugenia. As he drove toward the church, Bart thought of the hundred kind things Martha had done for him. Things done without extracting a promise of restitution. His eyes blurred. There was no way to thank her now. He took a deep breath and drove on.

Bart knew what was ahead. Martha would be washed in lye soap and dressed by the ladies. She would lie on the bed for a day or so until whatever family there was could gather and the grave digger could do his work. Friends would come to the house and pay their respects. Flowers would fill the room, and perfume would be dabbed onto Martha. Food would accumulate. Coffee and sweet tea would be drunk by the gallon. Old memories would be woven into stories of her. There would be a graveside service of praying and singing. Cyrus would order her a nice stone from the mason with her name spelled out in big letters. Folks would bring flowers to lay on her box.

Cyrus and Eugenia sat at the kitchen table and listened to the church music, praying and preaching. Both thought about turning the Radiola box off, but neither could deal with the opaque silence. Neither wanted to talk of their feelings for fear that one would kick off the other into a crying jag.

"I'll pour myself a cup of coffee," Cyrus finally said. "Do you want one?"

"No thanks. I'm fine."

"I figure this is going to be a long day. Do you think you can help me through it?"

"I'll do what I can. I'm not feeling all that strong. When Bart gets back with the preacher, I'll feel a lot better."

"I'm thinking you and Bart should get married right off after the… after your mother's services, I mean. I think she would have wanted it that way. You know, get some celebrating in right after the grieving to wash it away and all. She was like that you know. She never cared about herself because she was always busy caring about others."

"Daddy. Stop talking like that, please. I'm just not ready to think about it right now. Maybe a walk would do us some good."

"You could pick her some flowers like you used to do when you were a little girl. I think she would like that."

"I can't think about marrying right now. It makes me think of her sitting in her chair stitching on my wedding dress. It's… not easy right now."

"You could probably take your mother's wedding dress to Stella Cohen and have it fitted to your body."

"I can't think of it."

"The next few days are going to be crazy." They walked out the kitchen door. "We'll have to shut the mill down and send the helpers off. Do you have mourning cloths?"

"No."

"You're going to need to go to the Cohens anyhow. Might

as well take the dress with you. I'm sure it will need to be freshened up some. Martha boxed it and stored it up in the attic somewhere. She probably sprinkled camphor or mothballs in the box with it. We had some photographs taken of us on our wedding day. I swear my feet never did touch the ground. I was floating like an angel. When we get back to the house, I want to get the photographs out. She was the prettiest thing I ever saw. I knew right off she was the one… like she was waiting for me to find her. She knew it too." Cyrus looked up at the sky and searched the clouds. "I don't know if you believe in that kind of stuff, but Martha claimed Cupid shot arrows at us. And now she is gone. Oh lord, what am I going to do?"

"Dad? I think we've got enough flowers." Eugenia played with the petals on the buckeyes. "Bart will be coming back with the preacher soon. We ought to be there so she isn't left alone."

"Thank you."

"For what?"

"Just being here with me. You're all I've got left of her."

"I'll always be here for you."

Cyrus put his arm around her shoulder. Together, they walked back to the house.

Eugenia sighed, "We got to get ready for all the visitors. I'd better straighten up the house."

"A herd of gaggling heifers, that's what they are. You can put as much distance between me and them as you want."

"They'll make conversation among themselves. You can count on that."

"They'll be talking about how Martha kept house for months until someone else dies."

"They mean good. They'll keep your mind off of things."

"I doubt it. All they'll talk about is Martha. Most of them didn't give a tinker's damn while she was alive. Now, they're going to rush in my home and… and whatever."

"Don't be so down on them. You can tolerate them for a day or so; then it will be all over."

"Maybe for them. It won't be over for us."

"Remember. They're our customers. They buy our flour and meal. They give us a living. Don't bite the hands that feed you."

Cyrus thought for a second. "If Martha were here, she could tell us if that came from the Bible or is a Chinese proverb. I'll miss her filling in the facts on matters. What are we going to do with all her books?"

"We could give them to the school library. Bart could stand to read a few to broaden his perspective of the world."

"He could do with some schooling that's for sure. Let's not fault him. Your mother wouldn't allow it. To her, he's genuine pure gold. I think he was the third love of her life, behind us."

"Here he comes now. Promise me you won't talk about our marriage. Let mother have her time. She deserves the attention, not Bart and me."

"I promise."

Bart leaped from the car. He addressed Eugenia, "The Jolly preacher man is on his way. He was still down at the church with Mr. Oliver counting the monies from the offerings and all." Turning to Cyrus, he informed him, "Mr. Oliver said he would pass along the word to the ladies of the church. They'll be along directly. Is there anything else I can do?"

"No," Cyrus said. "Why don't you come sit with us till Reverend Jolly arrives. You didn't have your coffee yet or any dinner. Maybe Eugenia can scratch us something to eat."

"What would y'all like? There's ham, eggs …."

"That would be just fine. Fry up some ham and eggs for us," Cyrus suggested. "And see if there are any biscuits left from breakfast."

"Is that okay with you, Bart," she asked.

"Oh yes, that would be just fine. Really anything will do. You know me. I ain't 'tickler when it comes to vittles." He paused then said, "I feel like I ought to be doing something."

"Would you like to put those flowers in water? That would be nice. You can put them on the stand next to Mother."

"Dad, you want the eggs scrambled or fried?"

"Scrambled will be fine, right alongside of the ham."

"Put the flowers on the counter, we'll take them to her after we eat. I'm only cooking enough for us, so if Reverend Jolly shows up, I'm not cooking for him too. I'd be in the kitchen cooking all day to fill him up."

"He's a big'un all right," Bart added.

"Eat as fast as it comes off the stove," Cyrus said.

Bart put water in a glass and stuck the flowers in but paused at the doorway. He went back to the kitchen. "Would you come with me?" he asked Eugenia.

"In a minute. I don't want to leave these eggs. If I get distracted, I burn them for sure. I can't seem to keep my mind on what I'm doing as it is. There aren't any more biscuits. Bart, pour us some tea from the pitcher, the one with the dishrag over it. The other one has clabbered biscuit milk in it. We can go in a minute. I want to draw the drapes and light some scented candles in the bedroom."

"We got to get us a lawyer," Cyrus said. "Something is supposed to be published in the paper. And, I think, a judge is supposed to sign some papers. Who does the death certificate?"

"Beats me," Eugenia answered.

"I'm most positive the preacher man goes through this regular like. He knows." Bart sat at the table and began to cut at his slab of ham.

"Maybe we ought to say a grace," Cyrus suggested. "Just on account of… you know." His head jerked up. "Lordy, I hear someone coming down the drive. Quick, Eugenia! Run out there and stall them till we can get something in our stomachs."

"Amen," Bart said just before he shoveled the eggs into his mouth. He reached for his tea glass to wash down the hastily-chewed food.

Cyrus dusted his eggs with salt and pepper and unfolded his napkin into his lap, confident that he would finish his dinner undisturbed. No one would dare encroach upon his privacy without first being greeted at the door and be invited into his home. No one would be as bold as Henslowe.

"I've got to see Bart. We have business that needs tending. He's expecting me. I'll show myself in." Henslowe took giant strides. Eugenia ran behind him.

"But… " Eugenia protested.

"Time is wasting young lady. I'd be much obliged if you would step aside."

Henslowe pulled at the screen door. He knocked once as he pushed the kitchen door open. "Well, howdy gents, Bart and Cyrus. I'm pleased to catch you. Um, that smells mighty fine - ham and eggs."

Neither were about to set a place for him. They looked up briefly, then continued to eat in silence. Neither gave him the courtesy of standing and shaking his hand. Eugenia stepped into the kitchen behind him.

"I tried to tell him, but he just pushed his way past me," Eugenia explained while thrashing her arms. She was flustered by his brashness.

"No matter," Cyrus said. "Take a seat, Reverend."

She thought, "If I were a man, I would have boxed him in the nose." Eugenia slammed her fist in her hand, making a clapping noise that drew attention.

"Don't you worry yourself about us eating in peace and quiet. Maybe the Reverend can do us a little favor while he's here." Cyrus handed Allston Henslowe the glass of flowers from the counter. "Would you make yourself useful until we finish off our dinner? Take these to Martha. She's been asking about them. She's in the bedroom."

Bart looked up sheepishly from his plate. Eugenia's eyes widened; her mouth fell open. "Dad!" she abruptly exclaimed.

In a moment Reverend Henslowe returned. His face was blanched. "Excuse me, Mr. Boyd, but it appears that Mrs. Boyd is sleeping."

"You don't say? Well let me wake her for you. I know you want to pay your respects to the lady of the house." Cyrus yelled,

"Martha, the Reverend Allston Henslowe brought you some posies. Martha, do you hear?" Cyrus looked back at Henslowe, "You know she's been feeling poorly. She needs all the rest she can get. But I know if she knew you were here, she would want to make you feel welcome by sharing our dinner with you."

"Oh Mr. Boyd, that isn't necessary. I hardly have an appetite today." Henslowe took off his hat and fumbled with the brim. His black hair was parted above the ear and pulled across his bald dome.

"Martha, the Reverend Henslowe wants something to eat. Come on in here, and fix him a plate. He said your ham and eggs smelled fine," Cyrus bellowed.

"Maybe you ought to go back and nudge her a bit to get her up and at your cooking. I imagine you have a healthy appetite that needs to be satisfied."

"Mr. Boyd, I do hate to wake her from her deep sleep."

"She isn't sleeping, only resting a little. I don't know how women know this sort of stuff, but she told me you would be coming by here today. I should send you on in to give her a good shaking to get her up."

"Now, you just go give her a shake like she said for you to do," Cyrus persisted. "Go on and don't forget her flowers. She was expecting them."

"Dad, how could you?" Eugenia spit the words out like they were scorching her tongue.

Bart poured himself another glass of tea. His hand was unsteady. He didn't want any part of Henslowe or the game Cyrus was playing. He wasn't going to take a side, make a comment, or look at anything in the kitchen but his empty plate. He fiddled with the fork and took another sip of tea.

"Give her a good shake Reverend. She's a heavy sleeper."

"Mr. Boyd?" Henslowe called from the bedroom.

"Give her a good shake, like I said," Cyrus answered.

"Mr. Boyd? Can you come here?" Henslowe called.

"Okay. I'll be there in just a second. Did you give her the flowers like I told you?"

"I put them on the night table."

Cyrus went to the room. "Eugenia, get the sheriff! This preacher killed your mother." Cyrus screamed at the top of his voice. "Get the sheriff. He strangled her with his bare hands."

Eugenia slammed the kitchen door Henslowe had left open.

"Mr. Boyd! I was only admiring her necklace. I swear, I never… I mean …. Mr. Boyd, I must sit down."

"Yup, she dead all right. You were the last one in the room. You did it. You took her life away from her just like you were trying to take her necklace. You're going to spend the rest of your days in jail. They might hang you in the square by the courthouse. The sheriff is on the way to get you now. You better pray, and I mean pray hard. I'm going to lock you in this room with her until he gets here to arrest you for murdering my wife. I'm going to be right outside the door with my shotgun in case you try to sneak out."

"But Mr. Boyd… "

Cyrus returned to the kitchen. "I ought to ask him about those bees while I have him in there."

"What do you plan to do?" Eugenia asked.

"Just sit here quiet like. He'll open a window and run off. And if we're lucky, we'll never see or hear from that scoundrel again."

Bart tried not to smile. He pursed his lips. Eugenia took a chair at the table.

"Where is my shotgun? I ought to let out a blast. That buzzard will think I'm shooting at him."

"What about his car?" Bart asked.

"You need one. Help yourself. He won't be back for it."

Cyrus went to the door and let out a shotgun blast, then another in the sky from his double-barrel 12-gauge. He could see something frantically cavorting in the brush down the road from the house. "Eugenia, go close the window in the bedroom. Bart, take that old rattletrap down to the mill and park it under the shed. Don't leave the key in it." Cyrus mumbled to himself,

"I never did like that man. Good riddance once and for all. I'll make apologies to your mother later. I bet there's a smile on her face now."

CHAPTER FOURTEEN

Reverend Homer Jolly came tumbling down the drive in his old jalopy. Although the car had been built as a Stanley Steamer, somebody replaced the steam drive with a gasoline motor. Gas cars started right off; steamers took a while. Most farmers preferred the steam engine on their tractors since it cost much less to operate. All you had to do to keep one going was to toss some dry kindling into the burner and top out the water tank at the well. Gas had gone up to seven cents a gallon. Gas engines would run off still juice if diluted with kerosene. Most farmers hated to waste good shine on an automobile unless they were racing; that's altogether different.

"Bart asked me to come by the house and see about Miss Martha," Reverend Jolly softly spoke.

Cyrus frowned, "She's passed on, and I think you might want to say a few words before she gets cold."

"You know I'm awful sorry to hear of this. I'm sorry for both of you. She was a fine woman, wife, and mother."

"She wasn't much for church, you understand," Cyrus added.

"From what I have been told, she had a saintly heart and a fear of the Lord. I don't believe that a person is a sinner if they don't go to church. If they have given their soul to the Lord, they will have grace and eternal salvation."

"I'm pleased to hear you speak of her that way. She read the Bible daily and could match anyone verse for verse on quoting scripture. I'd like for you to place her Bible in her hands before you say your prayer over her. She's in the bedroom. I'll walk you in and leave the two of you in private."

Cyrus closed the door behind Reverend Jolly and returned to the kitchen. In a few minutes Reverend Jolly joined him. "I need to get your approval on the arrangements," Jolly asked.

"You and Eugenia work out what you need to do. Whatever arrangements are made are fine with me."

"Is there anything special, like maybe a favorite hymn?" Jolly asked.

Cyrus answered, "Not that I can think of. She was a plain and simple person."

"Mr. Oliver said he would pass the word around to the ladies."

"I'm sure they will know what to do."

Cyrus turned to Bart, "Would you mind picking out a nice box for Martha?"

"No sir, not a bit. I'd be honored."

"I don't mean a pine box, but nothing too fancy. Make sure it has a good lining in it."

"Yes, sir. And a soft satin pillow."

The women came to the house and tended to Martha. She was placed in the box and taken to the church early the next morning. The grave diggers made haste. By noon the viewing was over and the hymn singing, praying, preaching, and saying of remembrances started. Of Martha's three older sisters, only Loula Roundtree was able to come to Butler to console the Boyds. Beulah and Eula were many years senior to Martha and were in the feeble years of their lives. By 3:00 Martha was being covered with red clay. The house was open to friends, family, and visitors.

Cyrus cornered Reverend Jolly. "What do I owe the church for all that was done?"

"Really, you only need to take care of the casket and diggers. $200 would suffice."

"I'd like to give $500 and for the balance going to the church organ fund."

"That's generous of you. Thank you. Everyone will benefit from Martha's memorial, and maybe some will add to it. You never know."

"I've been meaning to ask you about Bart being baptized. I think we should do it right away. Martha wanted him and Eugenia to marry this fall, but with all that's been going on, the two of them haven't set a date. Maybe you can have a talk with the boy and tell him what he's supposed to do next. He doesn't have any family but Eugenia and me, and we should be the last ones to tell him what to do."

"I'll have a word with him."

"Don't mention that it was my suggestion. This conversation is just between the two of us and never needs to go any further. I'm talking for what's best for my daughter, you understand. I just want Eugenia to have a happy life; she deserves it. I had to hold her back to help me with the mill. If Bart could take over with a couple of hired hands, then she could stay home and have babies. That would have made Martha so happy."

"It's not Martha, or you for that matter, that should deal in the happy business. Patience is a virtue. Like the path of the New River, in due time nature will take a wish in a bottle along her meandering course to the sea. Let's let nature take her own natural course with them."

"Your saying Bart is the wish and Eugenia is the bottle?"

"It could be the other way around, you know."

"All I'm asking is an estimate of when that bottle will reach the sea. I know it is in the river someplace. I don't want it hung up in some branch or stranded on a sandbar. A little nudging wouldn't hurt what nature has planned, now would it?"

Eugenia approached. Suspiciously she asked, "What are you men talking about?"

Reverend Jolly answered, "Sugar, your dad and I were talking about going fishing on the New River for one of those monster bed cats. I've heard it told that they make beds in rock fissures and lay there with their mouths open for ten years sucking up food. They get so large a man can put his arm through the gill and out the mouth and the fish will swim him downstream for days."

"You men, always thinking about fishing or hunting the impossible dream."

"Sugar, dreams come true only when they are pursued; otherwise they will always remain a dream and nothing more," Jolly added.

"You might as well hunt unicorns than catfish as big as an outhouse. Besides, everybody knows the bigger they grow, the tougher the meat. One that size would be good for nothing but parading around to show folks."

Cyrus added, "It would feed many a cat."

"You would have to have a wagon and a team of mules to pull it around. And who do you think would help you load it?" Eugenia rebuffed.

"Wouldn't matter much. Everybody would pay a dime to see it," Cyrus persisted.

"In a week, it would stink so bad people would pay you to throw it back in the river."

Cyrus continued, "Women! They are so practical. They have answers for everything. I think if the Wright brothers had wives, planes wouldn't have been invented. I can hear them now, 'You'll never get that glued-up pile of wood and cloth off the ground. It'll never fly.' Poof! There goes another dream."

"If the two of you want to go fishing so bad, get on over there to the mill pond with a bucket of worms or crickets. Ed Watson pulled a ten-pound bass out of there last week. His fish could feed a family of four and all his cats. Y'all catch a mess, and I'll fry them."

"You got yourself a deal," Jolly said. "Oh, by the way. Does your Bart need to be baptized?"

"An immersion wouldn't do him any harm," Eugenia answered.

"Why don't we put it on the church calendar?" Jolly suggested.

Bart approached. Innocently he asked, "What are y'all talking about?"

The Reverend Jolly answered, "Mr. Boyd has made a generous contribution to the organ fund as a memorial to Miss Martha. We were wondering if you would like to sing in the choir after it is installed."

"Me sing in a choir! I can hardly whistle a tune."

"We can teach you to make a humming noise in the background until you get the hang of it. But I think you should be a church member first."

"You gotta be a church member to hum in the choir?" Bart asked.

"Well, it is customary. Maybe we could take you on a trial basis."

"I won't do it unless Eugenia does it with me."

"Then it's settled. First, you become a member of the church, then we'll give you humming lessons."

Cyrus had to turn away or else he would burst out laughing. Jolly lived up to his name. The guy was pulling Bart's leg clean off his hip. Eugenia took Bart's hand.

"That would be wonderful," Eugenia said.

"On a trial basis. If'n it don't work out, there won't be no hard feelings, will there?"

"Oh, not at all. We have members of the church who are on a list waiting for voice lessons. It might be years before we can help them learn choir singing. But Bart, I think you have potential. I think you have a natural baritone voice which would complement the sound of the choir. Your voice is what is missing. For that reason, I'll put your name at the top of the list."

"You don't have to be in such a gall darn, excuse me I forgot you were a preacher man, hurry to put me ahead of people that's been waitin' fer years. They'd get mad at my cuttin' in front of them."

Cyrus stepped back after pretending to have a cough. He pulled his handkerchief from his back pocket.

Still managing to keep a straight face, the Reverend Jolly continued, "Oh, no. Not at all. Let me explain. Some on the list are children. If they were in the choir, they would fidget and twist and look all about. They wouldn't sit still. When I'm in the middle of a sermon, they get bored, and the congregation watches them instead of listening to the word of the Lord. Now then, there's the old folks. They have a tendency to cough and sneeze, which just won't do at all. The old men fall asleep during my sermon. If you were a member of the congregation listening to a sermon, would you want some old man coughing and sneezing and snoring during the sermon?"

Cyrus pulled his handkerchief from his pocket and again stepped away. His faux cough had returned with a vengeance.

"No sir."

"Well, there you have it. That's why you will be at the top of the list."

"I never thought about it that away."

"There are just some things you have to do in life just because they are right and for no other reason. You show up Sunday, and I'll give you a pamphlet to study that explains what being a member of a church is all about. The following Sunday, week after next, I'll ask you questions from the pamphlet so I know you have studied at being a Christian. The following Sunday, after services, we'll have your Baptism and a celebration picnic. The Sunday after that I'll announce to the congregation that you have fulfilled all your obligations of wanting to be a Primitive Baptist Christian, and they will take a vote on giving you a church membership. Then and only then, can you receive your humming lessons."

Tears were forming in Cyrus' eyes above his handkerchief. His cough was drawing Eugenia's attention.

"You all right, Dad?" she asked.

"Just give me a minute," he responded with great difficulty.

"Have all the choir members gone through all them procedures?"

"Every last one of them, without exception."

Eugenia reassured Bart, "I would be so proud of you if

you did all Reverend Jolly says."

"You've done it too?" Bart asked Eugenia.

"Yes. I have, before I met you."

"But you're not a member of the choir?"

"But I will be after your lessons."

"Well, okay. I guess so. Sure seems like a big to-do over nothing."

"When you read the pamphlet, it will explain away most of your doubts. You'll see."

Seth and Azalee Palmer waved as they walked to their car. Mary and Terry Goddard were in the yard talking to Aunts Carlotta and Loula. Some of the church women were still in the house cleaning up plates and dishes. They consolidated the abundant gifts of food and sang as Ed played hymns on his accordion. Evening was beginning to set in. The tree frogs and crickets were beginning their nightly ruckus.

"I best be gettin' to my place and see 'bout things thar," Bart suggested to Eugenia. "I know you and Mr. Boyd needs your time together."

"Oh, you needn't go just yet. Did you have a slice of Mary Goddard's chocolate cake?"

"I et so much I could pop my buttons. Every time I turnt around someone was passing me a plate full of something. I must'a et three dinners till I had to git away from the kitchen. Think it'd be all-right if'n I take Reverend Henslowe's car back to the house? Mr. Boyd said I should have it."

"If my dad said it was yours for the keeping, then you best take it out of his sight. I'll see you at the mill."

"Okay. Good night."

"Bart? I want you to give me a little kiss goodnight."

Bart walked up real close to Eugenia. "You mean right here in front of your dad and the preacher man?"

"Especially right now."

"Well, okay." Bart leaned to Eugenia's waiting lips and gave her a little peck. His face was crimson.

"That was nice," Eugenia said.

Bart shook the hands of Mr. Boyd and Reverend Jolly and walked to the mill.

Eugenia watched him walk away then she turned to Reverend Jolly and her father. "I can't believe the two of you. What you are trying to do is good, but I think your methods are reprehensible. You both treat him like he is a little boy."

The Reverend Jolly responded, "I'm pleased that you are going to join the choir."

"What could I do? Show him what a fool the two of you made him out to be? I only went along with the ruse because the truth would have hurt the two of you worse. If he finds out how you've played with him, he'd walk away from the church just like mother did. I don't want that to happen to anybody else. I hope you understand. I won't put up with it."

Eugenia indignantly strutted to the house.

"Humming lessons. That was a pretty good one," Cyrus commented.

Cyrus and the Reverend walked to the kitchen side porch chairs and took a seat beside one another.

Jolly responded, "I've got forty other ways to get people in church. I'll use them all if I have to. I'm just as mule-headed as your daughter. You and I are going to get the two of them married in a proper church ceremony, and that's that, or there ain't going to be a winter."

"Did you hear the way that boy profaned? 'Gal darn' is the first cousin to blasphemy. We got to fast-track him to salvation while we still have time. He could go the other way. All men are weak and easily enlisted in Satin's army."

"I didn't think there was an emergency." Cyrus pondered for a second. "He did seem reluctant though."

"We all have that internal battle of good and evil, right and wrong. The struggle is as old as man. Only salvation by confession can tip that scale in his favor."

"You're a good preacher. I appreciate your taking an interest in the boy. He'll turn out to be a fine man if we can hone down his rough edges."

"Oh, I have no doubt he will grow into a man you will be proud to call son-in-law. After we get him baptized and accepted as a member of the church, we can start working on the wedding date. I've got a bag of tricks for that too."

"Eugenia has been working on his civilized manners. You should have seen his dancing lessons. I fell out of my chair laughing. I wouldn't miss his humming lessons for anything in the world. He's a challenge all right. You know the loss of Martha has suffered me. But the joy that boy brings to my life, well, I don't know how to describe it. He's like a little puppy. He gnaws with sharp teeth and isn't always focused on what he's doing, but he has potential, like you said, to be a fine young man. I'm happy Eugenia picked him out."

"The Lord works in mysterious ways," Jolly summarized.

"Isn't that the truth. At first sight, I nearly ran him off as a no-good cur dog."

"We're going to make a fine Christian out of him, in spite of his reluctance."

"I appreciate all you are doing, not only for him but for all of us. Did I tell you I ran that Henslowe off with a shotgun yesterday?"

"I can't say I'm proud of you. But I think you did the right thing."

"I hope he keeps running and doesn't stop till he reaches the Ocean of Bengal. Martha would know where that is. I'm sure going to miss her."

"It's hard to say what your future will be like. Only you can determine which way you will go. Always remember to keep the church as part of your life, and you will have sure footing."

"With Eugenia and Bart, I'll be right there," Cyrus said with chipper enthusiasm. With a more foreboding expression, he continued, "The next six months are going to be a real challenge though. I know I should mourn Martha, but her loss was the end of lingering… you know what I mean. She was ill for a long time. Passing was a relief to her. I'm thankful she's no longer suffering. We danced the night before she …. It was almost like she knew and wanted the last moment together to be a happy one for me to remember." Tears filed Cyrus' eyes. "We had a good life together. She was the love of my life."

"Just you wait until you hold their little baby in your arms," Jolly said. "The world will have a whole new look."

Cyrus looked out over the pond toward the mill. "Having a grandson," he thought.

"I hate that Martha will miss that."

"She'll be looking down on him. Don't you worry about that. She'll be all over that child. Just wait; you'll see her face in the infant plain as day."

CHAPTER FIFTEEN

Cyrus didn't feel well. He had a fretful night's sleep, being up and down most of the night. Maybe, he thought, he had eaten a few too many of the wrong things that had been left at the house, maybe he was beginning a cold. He didn't complain to Eugenia after he slowly walked down to the mill. Eugenia told him Martha's monument had been placed at the grave site. The bill had been hand delivered to her at the mill that morning.

"Let's go to the church cemetery and look at her monument," Eugenia suggested.

"No. I'd rather rest today. I've been feeling kind of peaked. We can go tomorrow. That stone isn't going anywhere."

"I'm going to run over there anyway just to make sure they spelled mother's name correctly. You never know. I told the man I want it to be right before I pay the bill."

"Go on then. I'll go later." Cyrus sat at his desk and shuffled bills. He could feel the vibration of the roller stone as he sat in his chair. He thought Bart would make a good miller. He couldn't get up the energy to go tell him. He felt drained and tired. The ordeal of the prior week seemed to have finally settled the weight upon him.

His eyes closed. The familiar vibration and sound wove a blanket of peace. They wrapped serenity around him and saturated him with the security a baby would find cuddled at a mother's breast. He dreamed of sitting in the kitchen sipping coffee in the early morning light. Martha had her back to him. She was busy at the stove. He saw her apron strings tied around her tiny waist in a drooping yellow bow. His mind made the apron new and the bow loops stiff with starch and wrinkle-free from ironing. Her hair was held up by black, shiny bobby pins. He could see the smoothness of her neck. She was twenty-something again. Her skin was fresh and soft. Her hair was brown. He reached to touch. His arm lifted in sleep as in the dream. He knew she would turn to him, and he would kiss her cheek. He could smell her feminine fragrance and warmth. He circled her waist with his arms and could feel the baby inside of her. His face smiled. Their hearts beat as a single song of joy.

"Mr. Boyd?" Cyrus could hear his name. The sound was coming from outside of the kitchen. He dreamed somebody wanted him down at the mill.

"Mr. Boyd?" The voice was not familiar. It wanted to pull him away from his embrace, from Martha.

"Mr. Boyd?" The voice was closer, inside the kitchen. The voice had no continuity to the picture, the sound, to the vibrations lulling him to Martha.

"Mr. Boyd?" The voice was an errant housefly persistently buzzing at his ear. He tried to swat at it to make it go away.

"Mr. Boyd?" The fly had landed on his shoulder and shook with force beyond the capabilities of a fly.

"I'm going to get the fly-swat after you if you don't go away," Cyrus spoke from his dream.

"Mr. Boyd there's man here to see you. I would have got miss Eugenia but she's gone off somewhares."

Cyrus opened his eyes. His dream evaporated. The vivid picture of Martha had evaporated.

"He's from the gov'ment and wants to inspect the dam," Jason reported. "Mr. Bart is busy at the grist. He says, 'No gov'ment man is gonna make him stop.' He says, 'If he stops, they won't get their revenue.' You're the onlyest one that can talk with him.'"

Cyrus sat up, turned to Jason and with a bellicose voice growled, "Why don't you show him where the dam is?"

"He seen it from the back side. Now, he wants a flat-bottom to check it from the front. We ain't got no boat."

"Tell him he should have brought his own and he can paddle all over the lake till his hands are blistered," Cyrus spoke abruptly to Jason being resentful he had been awakened from his dream.

"Yes sir, Mr. Boyd."

"Damn them all. A man can't have any peace and quiet when he wants to," Cyrus thought to himself.

He pushed himself from his repose and followed Jason from his office. Two men, one with a clipboard, stood by the scales. "What can I do for you gentlemen?"

"We're here to inspect the mill." The taller of the two did the talking.

"All of it or just some of it?" Cyrus asked, obviously annoyed by their intrusion.

"The state sent us out to inspect your dam. When was it built?" the same official asked.

"The year of the centennial, 1876. My father used the best cement and steel in the construction. It's guaranteed to last for a hundred years. The Romans built with cement and no steel, and their buildings are a 1000 years old."

"The Romans didn't build your dam. We have to look it over all the same."

"Go right ahead. I usually charge a quarter a person, but I reckon you fellows aren't used to having to make a productive living. You spend the tax dollars I make, so be quick about it, then get on your way. I'm not going to give you any free samples either. Get on with your do-nothing jobs and don't come back till 1976. Jason, you go along with them in case one of them falls into the pond and can't swim out." Cyrus walked back to his office without giving them any further attention.

Cyrus knew they looked Republican, poking into his business for no-good reason other than knowing he had always voted Democrat. Cyrus wanted to go back to the house to finish his dream. It wasn't much of a day. The sky was miles thick with heavy grey clouds. The humidity was high, meaning the milling stone furrows would get all gummed up and have to be cleaned often. Cyrus didn't have the energy. His ache was private. He would take the day off from milling with hope he would heal.

Cyrus went to the house and sat in his kitchen easy chair facing the stove. He wanted his dream of Martha to come back.

Eugenia came abruptly in the door and reported the monument was perfect. "The name, inscription, and dates are correct, and it is placed at the head end of the gravesite. I'm amazed they got it right."

"The Moss brothers have had a hundred years of experience. There's no reason to think they would get it wrong."

"Well, it doesn't hurt to check. When you go, will you take some fresh flowers? I threw away all the wilted ones."

"We can't be going up there every day with flowers. They don't grow that fast."

"What got you so sour? Let me fix you a ham biscuit. If you ate something, you would feel better."

Eugenia took a biscuit from the breakfast tray, still warmed from the stove's lingering radiant heat. She sliced a biscuit-sized piece of salt-ham from the black iron fry pan.

Cyrus intently watched her at the stove. The vision was the same as his dream. She was the same size and shape as Martha. To Cyrus only a few minutes had passed when he felt Martha's belly swollen with child. "What happened?" he thought. He vaguely remembered Eugenia being a baby, a child. Shiny pools of fluid filled his eye crescents. She had grown to a woman in her mother's place. Eugenia placed the ham biscuit on a plate in front of Cyrus. She saw his tears fall down his cheeks.

Cyrus commented, "You ought to use an apron when you're at the stove, like …, like your mother."

"You're crying." Eugenia knelt down by his side and put her cheek next to his.

"She has her fragrance," Cyrus thought.

Eugenia kissed him on the cheek. His tears would not stop. Eugenia brought a framed photograph of Martha from the bedroom and placed it on the table by the ham biscuit. The red color of gingham oil cloth reflected onto the photograph. Her image appeared to be bleeding. Cyrus realized Martha missed him as much as he did her. Her torment of separation must be as painful as his own.

"Please no. Not yet. I know you mean well but I'm not ready. Give me a little time, and I'll be all right."

Eugenia had never seen her father cry. She had never seen tears form in his eyes and spill down his cheeks from the torment of life's sufferings. He had always seemed so strong. Before her was revealed a man who seemed weak and vulnerable. She wanted to hold him to make the pain go away. She wanted to console him with words of reassurance.

"I think I'll go lay down for a while. There were some men down at the mill inspecting the pond. You might want to check on them. Don't do them any favors, or they won't go away. I'll be down after I rest for a while."

Cyrus stretched out in the familiar bed. Where there were two now there was one. He thought the bed seemed so big and empty. The heartache didn't go away. Visiting the monument would not subdue his thoughts of Martha either.

"Yoo-hoo, anybody home?" There was a steady pattering at the kitchen door. Cyrus hadn't pulled his shoes off. He thought he recognized the voice to be Azalee Palmer. He rose to answer the persistent knocks and calls.

"Well, there you are, Cyrus Boyd. I was just passing by and thought I might make a call to see how you and Eugenia are fairing along all by the twosome. Do you have a list of things you need - coffee, sugar, detergent, and such like? You have to keep a list or, if you are like me, you'll come home and you've forgotten half of the things you meant to get."

"Oh, I don't really know. I think Eugenia is keeping up with the house supplies. We've got all the groceries we can use for a month. Thank you for all your kindness. I don't think we could have managed without your taking over the kitchen while we were receiving."

"Reverend Jolly mentioned you might need advice on the marrying off of Eugenia and her young beau. Azalee was adorned with a large and floppy wide-brimmed hat almost the size of a wash tub. It was as red as her lip color. "Has he asked for her hand?"

"Yes. A couple of times."

"That's wonderful. Then, all we need to do is set the date for them at the church. I'll order the invitations, and all we have to do is fill in the blank places."

"What do we need invitations for?"

"The wedding of course. Do you mind if I light a cigarette?"

"No. Go right ahead. Everybody will know to come to the wedding if we just tell them, won't they?"

"First, we put something in the newspaper; that makes the announcement official. Then, we start having little girl parties. Does she have a hope chest? A trousseau? Has she picked out her bridal gown?"

"We talked about her using her mother's dress."

"She'll have to take it to Stella Cohen for fitting, cleaning, and ironing."

"We already talked about that. But with the funeral and all... "

"I brought a little pocket calendar to make finding a date easier. Let's see... " She flicked an ash on the linoleum floor. Her lip color adhered to the cigarette pinched between her fingers. Her nails were the same gloss red as her lips and hat.

"We're talking about a fall wedding," Cyrus prompted.

"Perfect! I love weddings in the fall. How about between Thanksgiving and Christmas? How does that sound?"

"Just fine, but it's not me getting married. Don't you think... "

Azalee cut him off, "Don't let the youngsters do any of the thinking, or else they may change their minds. We want to make it easy for them. They just show up when and where we say. That's how it's done. When you were married, who made all the decisions?"

"I don't recollect."

"It's the bride's mother. That would have been Martha.

Everybody else does what they are told. Since Martha can't help us, we have to help ourselves to do what she would have done. Right?"

"Well, I guess so."

"Okay. Good. So, let's write down what we want to be in the paper. The first Saturday after Thanksgiving is December 6th. The next is the 13th. A lot of people are superstitious and won't come out of the house on that day."

"The 6th is fine."

"We are making progress here. I need Eugenia and Bart's full name for the invitations."

"Eugenia Marie Boyd and Bartholomew something Rombert."

"Is it spelled r-u?"

"No. That's capital R, little o-m-b-e-r-t, Rombert."

"Really, the only place it makes a whole lot of difference is on the marriage certificate and on the county record books. Okay, I count 13 weeks between now and the 6th. We have a lot of work to do in a short time. You better find that dress now so I can take it to Stella. It could be bug-eaten. I'll finish writing out the announcement while you find it."

In a few minutes, Cyrus returned from the attic with a box. Azalee opened it and unfolded the dress. "It looks perfectly fine to me. Stella will make it look new. Send Eugenia to her in a week for a fitting. By then she will have it cleaned and pressed."

"I was looking at Eugenia just this morning. I swear they are the same size. They could wear each other's shoes."

"She'll need new ones. Styles change so frequently. What was in fashion yesterday is out today. We don't want her looking like the cover of *Post* do we?"

"In about a month, you need to take them to the courthouse to get a marriage license. They can't be married without one. I think the fee is about $1.50 in cash."

"What else?" Cyrus asked.

"You've got to have a reception after the wedding. Do

you want it here or somewhere else? How many people are you inviting to the wedding? The more that come, the bigger the place."

"Bart doesn't have any family. We only have a few aunts and cousins out of town. So, mostly the people we invite will be from right around here."

"So, let's figure. How many farmers do you mill for?"

"Probably, about 200 give or take."

"How many families or stores do you sell to?"

"Oh, that would be another 50."

"How many suppliers do you buy from?"

"There aren't but about 10 of them."

"Now, how many are there at church that aren't on those three lists?" Azalee was writing down all these numbers as Cyrus recited them.

"That might be another 25 or so."

She added them up. "So, we need 300 invitations and room for 500 people including children. You can't get all that many people in your house at one time. We better rent the city building. Who are you going to get to do all the cooking and setting up of tables at the reception?"

"I haven't thought of that."

"Don't worry. Let me take care of that. I'll make sure to get Eugenia's okay on all the food. People usually want to eat a good meal rather than finger food. You've been to enough weddings to know what I'm talking about. There are good weddings, and then there are those wedding done on a shoestring budget. I think you want Eugenia to have a nice wedding reception rather than one with only nuts and punch."

"I guess so. But as I said, you need to check with her on some of these do and don't things."

"I will. That's about it. Oh, I almost forgot. We need to get Bart outfitted at Cohen's. Don't send him at the same time you send Eugenia for her fitting. It's not proper for the groom to see the bride in her gown before the wedding."

Azalee abruptly stood up. Cyrus rose quickly in response.

Azalee tucked her cigarettes package into a side pocket of her silk dress. It had a red floral pattern - maybe roses. Her girth was banded by a 6-inch black patent leather belt.

"I really appreciate your making this move along."

"Think nothing of it. I've got three daughters. None are over twelve yet, but this is good practice. Remember, the ladies are going to have some parties for Eugenia. See that she has nice dresses to wear. Mrs. Cohen will take care of everything." Azalee moved toward the kitchen door.

"I hope I can remember all you've said."

"I'll see you at church to nudge you along. So will all the ladies. They will make such a fuss over Eugenia you will think she is the Queen of England. The gentlemen will salute Bart. Seth will handle that part of it." She stepped out and strutted toward her car.

"Don't forget I need the names and addresses of all 300 people who are going to be invited. You better get busy on the list because you don't want to leave somebody out. That would be a terrible faux pas."

"I hope I can remember what to do first. Thirteen weeks you say?"

Azalee turned and reiterated, "That's right; 13 weeks. Remember: If you get stuck in a social tree, call Azalee."

She was departed in the same whirlwind as she had arrived.

All malaise feelings had left Cyrus. His mind was swept away from Martha's yellow apron. Azalee had restored his presence. He went to the mill and began to engage Eugenia with the conversation he had with Mrs. Palmer concerning the wedding arrangements but stopped short of actually telling her they had agreed upon a date. He had to make the date selection seem to be her suggestion in cooperation with Bart. He thought that casually bringing up the subject at supper would be more appropriate. Hopefully, if things went well at the mill, Bart could eat with them before the second crew arrived.

CHAPTER SIXTEEN

Grandfather Boyd gripped the knob of the cane tightly as he swung it around his head. Once he didn't, and it flew from his grip and broke a window. They all laughed at his antics, but he didn't see the humor invested in a story that ended with something broken. He felt humiliated they missed the point and were focused instead on the damage.

"Pa." Ted related to Bart, "He knocked a blade off the ceiling fan. He got all wound up on politics again. I got him and old Reverend Jolly talking about fishing, and they want you to get them some crickets for bait."

"Me! You get the crickets." Bart was going through the payroll records at his desk. The sleeves on his white linen shirt were rolled up his forearms. His tie was loosened and tucked into the shirt between buttons, army style. "You got them wanting to go fishing."

"If I hadn't, they would have torn the house apart. Where's Mother?"

"Darn if I know. She could be over at the cabin gettin' ready for camp meeting. Who knows? Say, while you're hangin' around here with nuthin' to do but gab, run out on the line and ask Windsor Forest fer his time sheets."

"Oh, dad. I got to get them in the boat with the poles, so they don't hurt nuthin' else," Ted argued. "Mom's going to fuss about the fan blade when she gets back. She gonna blame me for not watchin' them."

"Ted, your grandfather would'a broken that blade with or without you in the house. Now, get on out there and get the time sheets. I need them. Do as I ask and don't give me any more of that back talk, or I'll tell your ma you broke that fan blade and want to blame Cyrus for it."

"But Dad!"

"I mean it. And don't you go running off to the pond. I got ten more things for you to do when you git back with the time sheets. Ya hear me?"

Ted scrunched up his face. He was ten years old and out from school for the summer. All he wanted to do was get into mischief or goad Cyrus into a renewed version of an old story. They bonded thicker than a honeysuckle vine wrapped around a wild cherry sapling. They both acted like children. Ted had an excuse; he was a child. But Cyrus, on the other hand, needed pruning. That job was always left up to Eugenia to handle. Replacing the blade would keep the two of them busy for half a day or longer.

The mill was being run by the Frammel brothers, Jason and Jackson. Both had married, with Azalee's direction of course, and had started families of their own. Bart had added more pasture to his beef farming and was running Rombert's Abattoir and Butchery. That and the poultry processing business were prospering far better than the milling operation.

Honey production was holding its own ground. Bart had hired a hand, Roger Lineberger, to tend to his cattle and bees. The Linebergers lived in Bart's house rent-free in exchange for their services. Bart generally gave them a Christmas bonus for hauling the hives all over the state to pollinate various crops. The compensation was good since the bees boosted crop production by 30 percent. Bart gave the farmers a discount if they used his bees and brought their grain to him for milling.

Another war was brewing in Europe. Cyrus was on a rampage of national isolationism. The Democrats had finally taking over the White house from the Republicans. The church organ needed repairs which had been neglected since the fire swept through the sanctuary in 1931. The organ and pipes had been rescued but never sounded the same after the church was rebuilt. Some said they were warped. Cedric had died, and the organ repair fund was under the direction of the choirmaster.

Church membership was nearly 750 people.

"What took you so long?" Bart barked at Ted.

"Mr. Forest was busy, and I had to wait for him to finish."

"Busy at what?" Bart asked more civilly. His forehead was furrowed with questioning lines.

"Something was broken, a conveyor chain I think, and he had to fix it."

"Did you watch him so that next time you could fix it yourself?"

"Yes, sir. But I don't want to work there. It stinks."

"Stinks! You mean it smells like a skunk or it's a stinking way of making a living?"

"Like a skunk," Ted answered.

"Well son, that's the smell of money being made. You remember that if you can't fix a conveyor chain. The smell of money always stinks. Where is your sister?"

"I think she went with Mother."

"You best go back to the house and watch your grandfather. He might try to pull a chair under that fan. Make sure he has something for lunch."

"What about the other nine things you wanted me to do?" Ted asked.

Bart leaned back in his chair, "Your grandfather is number nine. When your mother gets back from camp, you come on back. I'll show you a chicken brought in this morning that has two heads."

"Show me now. I want to see it. Please," Ted begged. He pulled at his father's sleeve. "Where is it?"

"Hold your horses. The chicken is number ten. You got to do things in order. Can't skip over one thing to another. And right now you better go tend to your grandfather before he hurts himself or wrecks the place. That chicken will be here when you come back."

"Oh, okay. Promise?"

"Hey, have I ever let you down?"

"No sir."

"Well, don't you let me down neither. Now, skedaddle."

Ted put his arm around Bart's shoulder, "Can I have a puppy? Mr. Palmer has a basket full of them at his store. They're free."

"We'll talk about it when you mother gets back. You got to catch her in the right mood, you know. With Grandfather Cyrus bustin' the fan, right now might not be a good time to talk about gettin' a puppy."

Ted made a sad face.

"Having a puppy takes a lot of responsibility. I think you could do it if you put your mind to it."

"So, it's okay with you?"

"Sure. A boy always gets a puppy a year or two before getting his first gun."

"A gun! What kind?" Ted asked enthusiastically.

"Your mother doesn't approve of guns either. So, we have to be very cautious in the way we approach her."

"Can I have your gold one?"

"We have to start off small and work up to the big one."

"I heard momma tell the story of how you won it from the world's best shot. I told Johnny at school but he didn't believe me."

"That was the last time I ever shot in a match against another man. I promised him I would never shoot again, and I've kept my word. Now run along. I've got work to do here. We can talk about dogs and guns this evening after supper. Ask Grandpa to tell you about his old dog, Dispatch."

Ted gave Bart a loving hug with both arms before he ran back to the house. Bart sat alone in his chair contemplating the happiness Eugenia, Ted, and Little Martha had brought to his life. He thought back to the days when he was not much older than Ted, to the day when he buried his mother and father beneath the shade of the apple tree by his old home place. They both died one after the other from sickness. There weren't no one to tend to them but himself.

He remembered sitting in a chair wondering what he

should do. He remembered dragging them by the heels to the hole he dug. There was no box, only a tattered wool blanket to comfort them. He remembered the tears in his eyes as he reluctantly shoveled the red clay over them. Somehow, he was spared and was left to take care of himself. He swore Ted would never suffer alone as he had.

He wanted Ted's hug to last forever.